ALEXAN   D0524363   in 1925, the son
of a Sc   .... ᴀther. After one year
of studying at Glasgow University, he was called up for war
service in 1943, and joined the Royal Navy. He returned to
complete his degree three years later. Afterwards he travelled
in Europe, and settled down in Paris, where he edited *Merlin*,
an avant-garde literary journal. He also started his writing
career, producing work for the controversial publisher
Olympia Press, including the first version of *Young Adam* in
1954. His lifelong drug habit began in this period. He then
moved to the US, settling first in New York City, where he
worked on a scow on the Hudson River, then in California,
where the Beat community had relocated. It was during this
time that he wrote possibly his most famous novel, *Cain's
Book* (1961). He moved to London in the 1960s, where he
more or less ceased his writing activities and remained until
his death in 1984.

Young Adam

Alexander Trocchi

With an introduction by Stewart Home

ONEWORLD
CLASSICS

ONEWORLD CLASSICS LTD
London House
243-253 Lower Mortlake Road
Richmond
Surrey TW9 2LL
United Kingdom
www.oneworldclassics.com

This edition published in the UK by Calder Publishing Ltd, 2003
Published 1954 by Olympia Press, subsequently revised 1961
and published by William Heinemann and in paperback by New
English Library, 1966.
Later published by John Calder (Publishers) Ltd, 1983, Rebel Inc,
1997.
© Calder Publishers UK Ltd & Alexander Trocchi Estate, 1954,
1961, 1966, 1983, 1999, 2003.
This edition first published by Oneworld Classics Limited in 2008
Introduction © Stewart Home, 2008

Printed in Great Britain by CPI Cox & Wyman Ltd, Reading

ISBN: 978-1-84749-042-1

Young Adam

Introduction

ALEXANDER TROCCHI was born in Glasgow in 1925 and died in London in 1984. His life, as much as his writing, is the stuff of legend. Considered by many to be the most dissolute of the beats, for a time it looked like he was more likely to be remembered as "The Lord of Junk" than as a writer. Trocchi was notorious both for his prodigious chemical intake and pimping his wife Lyn to get money to pay for drugs. But times change and fashions do too; and now "Scots Alex", as Trocchi was known on the west London drug scene, has become an almost respectable literary figure.

For contemporary Scots writers Trocchi's immersion in the hippy counterculture makes him a more attractive literary figure than the country's other relatively visible modernists of the Fifties and Sixties, such as Edwin Morgan, Ian Hamilton Finlay and Hugh MacDiarmid (all principally poets). Irvine Welsh has been quoted as calling Trocchi "the George Best of Scottish literature". Other Scots writers owe even deeper debts to Trocchi; former boxer Barry Graham went as far as penning a Trocchi parody novel *The Book of Man* (1995). In London, where Trocchi settled in the early Sixties, he towers over those who might be seen as his most immediate English literary heirs, such as Ann Quin, B.S. Johnson and Alan Burns. Trocchi did little writing after washing up in London, but he cut a doomed and dashing figure hanging out with the likes of black power leader Michael Abdul Malik, and fellow beat generation stalwart William Burroughs.

There is considerable division over which Trocchi book is his best, but the consensus of opinion is either *Young Adam* (1954) or *Cain's*

Book (1961). *Young Adam* tends to catch the attention of those less interested in drugs and literary experimentation. To date this book has suffered from being seen as a work of late-modernism cast in the same mould as Beckett, Genet and Ionesco. Trocchi had a hand in publishing all three of these writers when he lived in Paris in the early to mid-Fifties.

Trocchi's importance as a proto-postmodernist has been obscured by what in retrospect appears an arbitrary division between his porn novels and "serious" works. In fact *Young Adam*, the earlier of his two "serious" novels, was first published under the pseudonym Frances Lengel as a "dirty book" by Olympia Press in 1954. The other titles written by Trocchi and published by Olympia under this name are *Helen and Desire* (1954), *Carnal Days of Helen Seferis* (1954), *School for Sin* (1955) and *White Thighs* (1955).

Trocchi re-edited *Young Adam*, removing a number of the erotic passages, so that it might be issued by a "reputable" publisher at a time when the use of extended pornographic tropes in literary novels had yet to become an accepted postmodern practice (cf. Kathy Acker, Bret Easton Ellis and Chris Kraus). What Trocchi excised from his "definitive" version of *Young Adam* were principally sex scenes, with one important exception. This is a climactic passage where Trocchi's narrator Joe recalls an argument with Cathie, his former lover, whose dead body he helps drag from a canal at the beginning of the book. Cathie is supporting Joe as he unsuccessfully attempts to complete a novel. Joe describes a day on which instead of writing he made custard, and when Cathie comes home this leads to a row. She refuses to eat the custard, so Joe throws it at her as she is taking off her work clothes, then he thrashes her with a rough slat of wood, before proceeding to tip ink, various sauces and vanilla essence over the girl:

I don't know whether she was crying or laughing as I poured a two-pound bag of sugar over her. Her whole near-naked body was twitching convulsively, a blue breast and a yellow and red one, a green belly, and all the colour of her pain and sweat and gnashing. By that time I was hard. I stripped off my clothes, grasped the slat of the egg crate, and moved among her with prick and stick, like a tycoon.

When I rose from her, she was a hideous mess, almost unrecognizable as a white woman, and the custard and the ink and the sugar sparked like surprising meats on the twist of her satisfied mound.

Trocchi is clearly using a fictional voice and, although it might be argued that he shares some of the Joe's misogyny, he was not prone to the racism implicit in the term "white woman". Likewise Trocchi's decision not to use Cathie's name at any point during his description of the "sploshing" and "thrashing" is clearly a conscious device aimed at revealing Joe's dehumanized "nature" as he reduces the object of his lust and fury to the same base level. This is just one of many passages that demonstrate Trocchi did not want Joe to be a sympathetic "character", or for the reader to trust him as a narrator. Joe's claim, sustained pretty much throughout the second and third parts of *Young Adam*, that Cathie met her death accidentally is not necessarily to be believed, just as at the end of *American Psycho* (1991) by Bret Easton Ellis the reader is left uncertain as to whether the narrator Patrick Bateman is a psychotic serial killer or a pathetic fantasist.

Another contemporary New York writer who retrospectively helps illuminate Trocchi's aesthetic stance here is Lynne Tillman. At the climax of her novel *No Lease On Life* (1998), the narrator Elizabeth Hall is so frustrated by her inability to find any peace in her Lower East Side apartment that she sends a rain of eggs splattering onto those making noise in the street below her. Tillman's book is loosely modelled on James Joyce's *Ulysses* (1922). The action takes place over twenty-four hours, but the tenor of the work and its denouement mark it as self-consciously postmodern. Tillman and Trocchi, who knew each other briefly, share a love of classic modernist literature, but at the same time both have moved beyond what even by the early 1950s was an exhausted literary form.

Trocchi's narrator, Joe, only admits that he knew Cathie halfway through *Young Adam*. Joe claims he'd wanted to focus on his attraction to his subsequent lover Ella, and therefore didn't explain how Cathie fitted into the overall picture of his life. At this point it is Joe and not the reader who has lost the plot. He is confused and says he killed Cathie: "There's no point in denying it since no one would believe me". To underline his sense of disorientation, Trocchi makes Joe speak of police "sensationalism" being reported in the newspapers, a reversal of commonplaces about "media sensationalism". The reader only has Joe's version of events, and Trocchi goes to great lengths to underline his unreliability:

It was an odd thing that I, who saw Cathie topple into the river, should have been the one to find her body the following morning at one mile's distance from where she fell in. I felt at the time that it was ludicrous, so incredible that if Leslie had not happened to come up on deck at that time I should most certainly have refused to accept such an improbable event and tried to thrust her away again with the boat hook.

While life is full of coincidences, the plots of novels are the result of conscious design. Most writers would avoid happenstances like the one Trocchi employs here, because although it just might occur in life, it isn't plausible as fiction. Trocchi, of course, uses it to undermine Joe's believability as a narrator. *Young Adam* has been called an "existential thriller" and compared to *The Outsider* (1942) by Albert Camus, but such descriptions rest on a misreading of Trocchi's text as being modernist. An unreliable narrator like Joe cannot be an existential protagonist because the philosophy of Jean-Paul Sartre, Albert Camus and their various followers is predicated on notions of authenticity. Joe is not even an authentic bargeman, he is a university drop-out who works on the canals for at most a few months.

Young Adam is neither an "existential thriller", nor merely a parody of that genre, but rather an entirely new type of work. Among the many indications that *Young Adam* is a postmodern fiction is the fading away of geographical descriptions as the book progresses. The first part of the narrative is a burlesque of exhausted modernist literature. Trocchi makes his prose deliberately awkward, thereby reversing the tactic he employed to parody pornography, which he wrote both too carefully and too well. Towards the end of *Young Adam* Trocchi has Joe tell us:

> I was out in the street early and found myself walking along Argyle Street in the general direction of the courts. I stopped for a cup of tea at a snack counter, smoked two or three cigarettes, and then continued on my way. As I walked through the town, a strange feeling of confidence settled upon me.

There is a pleasing vagueness to this passage, allowing the reader to draw their own associations from the name Argyle Street. Given that this is one of the longest boulevards in Glasgow – running from the High Street out to Kelvingrove Park in the west end – a conventional (as opposed to a pulp or postmodern literary) novelist would have described the section of the road they passed along in some detail. It should go without saying that Argyle Street today is very different to the one being invoked when these lines were written more than fifty years ago; to the east it is now littered with pound shops and dominated by the glass hulk of the 1980s St Enoch

11

Shopping Centre, while the M8 motorway completely separates that part of the avenue from the more residential section to the west. Notice also *Young Adam*'s trademark sloppiness in the passage quoted above, achieved via Trocchi's self-conscious repetition of words such as "street" and "walked/walking",

Returning to Joe, he is confident he won't have to answer to the police or courts (or indeed his less sophisticated readers) for killing Cathie. At the end of *Young Adam* an innocent man is condemned to death for the girl's murder; and Joe's cold psychotic nature is underlined by his reaction as he watches the drama unfold in court: "The man who was created in the speeches of the procurator was fitted admirably to the crime which the police had invented – a very gratifying thing indeed to see two branches of the public service, the judiciary and the police, work together in such imaginative harmony." Joe can't even stay on this train of thought; he breaks to write two sentences about playing pinball in a Jamaica Street dive, then returns to the courtroom to hear the inevitable guilty verdict on the innocent man. Joe is cast very much in the same mould as another of Trocchi's "anti-heroes", the murderous and lustful Saul Folsrom in *White Thighs*. Both these non-characters owe something to Lee Anderson, the narrator of Boris Vian's *I Spit on Your Graves* (1946).

I Spit on Your Graves was a literary hoax that was first published as if it had been written in English by an Afro-American author called Vernon Sullivan, and Vian was merely its translator. In fact there was no Vernon Sullivan, the ostensible author of this work was a figment of Vian's imagination and the book was written in French. Vian's first-person narrator, Lee Anderson, adopts a prose style and worldview heavily influenced by Henry Miller and James M. Cain. Although Anderson identifies himself as an Afro-American male, he is able to pass as white and revels in seducing privileged southern girls who have no idea that he is black. These sexual conquests are presented as a form of revenge against the white racists, who Anderson tells us murdered his darker-skinned brother. However, Anderson's sexual shenanigans are a mere prelude to him slaughtering two white sisters, Lou and Jean Asquith.

I Spit on Your Graves was hugely controversial and there was much speculation about its authorship until the hoax was finally revealed. Trocchi's greatest success through scandal in the dirty book business was a faked fifth volume of *My Life And Loves* (1959), supposedly written by the philanderer and literary middleman Frank Harris. Again this was Trocchi engaging in a burlesque – he disliked Harris as a middle-brow literary figure and, although the book was accepted as genuine upon publication, it was an opportunity for its real author to parody and pillory the man who was supposed to have written it. This is typical of Trocchi's approach to writing fiction, and the only real exception to it is *Cain's Book*, which in any case is fictionalized autobiography alchemized into an "anti-novel". The jury is still out on whether *Young Adam* or *Cain's Book* is Trocchi's greatest work but, regardless, the former remains the best introduction to his writing, because it is so much more typical of his proto-postmodernist approach.

– *Stewart Home, 2008*

Young Adam

Part One

1

T HESE ARE TIMES when what is to be said looks out of the past at you – looks out like someone at a window and you in the street as you walk along. Past hours, past acts, take on an uncanny isolation; between them and you who look back on them now there is no continuity.

This morning, the first thing after I got out of bed, I looked in the mirror. It is of chromium-plated steel and I always carry it with me. It is unbreakable. My beard had grown imperceptibly during the night and now my cheeks and chin were covered with a short stubble. My eyes were less bloodshot than they had been during the previous fortnight. I must have slept well. I looked at my image for a few moments and I could see nothing strange about it. It was the same nose and the same mouth, and the little scar above and thrusting down into my left eyebrow was no more obvious than it had been the day before. Nothing out of place and yet everything was, because there existed between the mirror and myself the same distance, the same break in continuity which I have always felt to exist between acts which I committed yesterday and my present consciousness of them.

But there is no problem.

I don't ask whether I am the "I" who looked or the image which was seen, the man who acted or the man who thought about the act. For I know now that it is the structure of language itself which is treacherous. The problem comes into being as soon as I begin to use the word "I". There is no contradiction in things, only in the words we invent to refer to things. It is the word "I" which is arbitrary and which contains within it its own inadequacy and its own contradiction.

No problem. Somewhere from beyond the dark edge of the universe a hyena's laugh. I turned away from the face in the mirror then. Between then and now I have smoked nine cigarettes.

It had come floating downstream, willowy, like a tangle of weeds. She was beautiful in a pale way – not her face, although that wasn't bad, but the way her body seemed to have given itself to the water, its whole gesture abandoned, the long white legs apart and trailing, sucked downwards slightly at the feet.

As I leant over the edge of the barge with a boathook I didn't think of her as a dead woman, not even when I looked at the face. She was like some beautiful white water-fungus, a strange shining thing come up from the depths, and her limbs and her flesh had the ripeness and maturity of a large mushroom. But it was the hair more than anything; it stranded away from the head like long grasses. Only it was alive, and because the body was slow, heavy, torpid, it had become a forest of antennae, caressing, feeding on the water, intricately.

It was not until Leslie swore at me for being so handless with the boathook that I drew her alongside. We reached down with our hands. When I felt the chilled flesh under my fingertips I moved more quickly. It was sagging away from us and it slopped softly and obscenely against the bilges. It was touching it that made me realize how bloated it was.

Leslie said: "For Christ's sake get a bloody grip on it!"

I leant down until my face was nearly touching the water and with my right hand got hold of one of the ankles. She turned over smoothly then, like the fat underbelly of a fish. Together we pulled her to the surface and, dripping a curtain of river-water, over the gunwale. Her weight settled with a flat, splashing sound on the wooden boards of the deck. Puddles of water formed quickly at the knees and where the chin lay.

We looked at her and then at each other but neither of us said anything. It was obscene, the way death usually is, frightening and obscene at the same time.

"A hundred and thirty at eleven pence a pound": an irrelevant thought... I didn't know how it came to me, and for more than one reason, partly because I knew Leslie would be shocked, I didn't utter it. Later you will see what I mean.

The ambulance didn't arrive until after breakfast. I don't suppose they were in a hurry because I told them she was dead on the telephone. We threw a couple of potato sacks over her so that she wouldn't frighten the kid and then I went over and telephoned and went back and joined Leslie and his wife and the kid at breakfast.

"No egg this morning?" I said.

Ella said no, that she'd forgotten to buy them the previous day when she went to get the stores. But I knew that wasn't true because I'd seen her take them from her basket when she returned. That made me angry, that she didn't take the trouble to remember how she'd examined the shells because she thought she might have broken one of them, and me there in the cabin at the time. It was a kind of insult.

"Salt?" I said, the monosyllable carrying the cynical weight of my disbelief.

"Starin' you in the face," she said.

It was damp. I had to scrape it from the side of the dish with my knife. Ella ignored the scratching sound and Leslie, his face twitching as it sometimes did, went on reading the paper.

It was only when I had began to eat my bacon that it occurred to me they'd had an egg. I could see the traces on the prongs of their forks. And after I'd gone all the way across the dock to the telephone... Leslie got up noisily, without his second cup of tea. He was embarrassed. Ella had her back to me and I swore at her under my breath. A moment later she too went up on deck, taking the kid with her, and I was left alone to finish my breakfast.

We were all on deck when the ambulance arrived. It was one of those new ambulances, streamlined, and the men were very smart. Two policemen arrived at the same time, one of them a sergeant, and Leslie went ashore to talk to them. Jim, the kid, was sitting on an upturned pail near the bows so that he would get a good view. He was eating an apple. I was still annoyed and I sat down on a hatch and waited. I looked out across the water at the black buffalo-like silhouette of a tug which crept upstream near the far shore. Beyond it on the far bank, a network of cranes and girders closed in about a ship. "To sail away on a ship like that," I thought, "away. Montevideo, Macao, anywhere. What the hell am I doing here? The pale North." It was still early and the light was still thin but already a saucer of tenuous smoke was gathering at the level of the roofs.

Then the ambulance men came across the quay and on to the barge and I pointed to where we had put the body under the sacks. I left them to it. I was thinking again of the dead woman and the egg and the salt and I was bored by the fact that it was the beginning of the day and not the end of it, days being each the same as the other as they were then, alike as beads on a string, with only the work on the barge, and Leslie to talk to. For I seldom talked to Ella, who appeared to dislike me and who gave the impression she only put up with me because of him: a necessary evil, the hired hand.

And then I noticed Ella pegging out some clothes at the stern.

I had often seen her do it before but it had never struck me in the same way. I had always thought of her as Leslie's wife – she was screaming at him about something or calling him Mister High-and-Mighty in a thick sarcastic voice – and not as a woman who could attract another man. That had never occurred to me.

But there she was, trying very hard not to look round, pretending she wasn't interested in what was going on, in the ambulance men and all that, and I found myself looking at her in a new way.

She was one of those heavy women, not more than thirty-five, with strong buttocks and big thighs, and she was wearing a tight green cotton dress which had pulled up above the backs of her knees as she stretched up to put the clothes on the line, and I could see the pink flesh of her ankles growing over the rim at the back of her shoes. She was heavy all right, but her waist was small and her legs weren't bad and I found myself suddenly liking the strong look of her. I watched her, and I could see her walk through a park at night, her heels clacking, just a little bit hurriedly, and her heavy white calves were moving just ahead of me, like glow-worms in the dark. And I could imagine the soft sound of her thighs as their surfaces grazed.

As she reached up her buttocks tightened, the cotton dress fitting itself to their thrust, and then she alighted on her heels, bent down, and shook the excess water out of the next garment.

A moment later she looked round. Her curiosity had got too much for her, and she caught me looking at her. Her look was uncertain. She flushed slightly, maybe remembering the egg, and then, very quickly, she returned to her chore.

The police sergeant was making notes in a little black notebook, occasionally licking the stub of his pencil, and the other cop was standing with his mouth open watching the stretcher-bearers who seemed to be taking their time. They had laid down the stretcher on the quay and were looking enquiringly at the police sergeant, who went over and looked under the sheet which they had thrown over her when they put her on the stretcher. One of them spat. I glanced away again.

Out of the corner of my eye I saw Ella's legs move.

Four kids from somewhere or other, the kind of kids who hang about vacant lots, funeral processions, or street accidents, stood about five yards away and gaped. They had been there almost since the beginning. Now the other policeman went over to them and told them to go away.

Reluctantly, they moved farther away and lingered. They grinned and whispered to each other. Then they whooped at the gesticulating cop and ran away. But they didn't go far, just round the corner of the shed across the quay, and I could see them poking their heads out round the corner, climbing over each other into sight. I remember one of them had flaming red hair.

The ambulance men had lifted the stretcher again but one of them stumbled. A very naked white leg slipped from under the sheet and trailed along the ground like a parsnip. I glanced at Ella. She was watching it. She was horrified but it seemed to fascinate her. She couldn't tear her eyes away.

"Woah!" the man at the back said.

They lowered the stretcher again and the front man turned round and arranged the leg out of sight. He handled it as though he were ashamed of it.

And then they hoisted the stretcher into the back of the ambulance and slammed the doors. At that moment Jim finished his apple and threw the core at the cat, which was crouched on its belly at the edge of the quay. The cat jumped, ran a bit, and then walked away with its tail in the air. Jim took out a tin whistle and began to play on it.

The sergeant closed his notebook, looped elastic round it, and went over to speak to the driver of the ambulance. Leslie was lighting his pipe.

Leslie had been a big man when he was younger, and he was still big at the time, but his muscles were running to flesh and his face was heavy round the chin so that his head had the appearance of a square pink jube-jube sucked away drastically at the top, and, as he didn't shave very often, the rough pinkness of his cheeks was covered by a colourless spreading bristle. He had small light blue eyes sunk like buttons in soft wax, and they could be kind or angry. When he was drunk they were pink and threatening. The way he was standing, running forwards and outwards from his razor-scraped Adam's apple to the square brass buckle of his belt, you could see he wasn't a young man; in his middle fifties, I suppose.

The ambulance was driving away and the sergeant was going over to talk to Leslie again. I remember it struck me as funny at the time that he should address all his remarks to Leslie. I watched the cat sniffing at something which looked like the backbone of a herring near the quay wall. It tried to turn it over with its paw. Then I heard Ella yelling at Jim. It seemed she hadn't noticed him before.

"I thought I told you to stay down below! I'll get your father to you!"

And then she turned on me and said I ought to be ashamed of myself for not keeping the boy out of the way. Did I think it was good for him to see a corpse? She said she thought I put the sacks over the body so as not to frighten him. I was about to say he didn't seem very frightened to me – sitting there playing "Thou art lost and gone forever, oh my darling, Clementine" on his tin whistle – but I could see she wasn't very angry. I could see she was in some way trying to get her own back for the long look I had at her backside, and that amused me and I didn't say anything. She turned away, lifted the basin which had contained the wet clothes, and I heard her clump down through the companionway into the cabin. Then, suddenly, I laughed. The kid was looking at me. But I went on laughing.

There was the discussion about suicide or murder. She asked him about it as soon as the police were gone, as soon as the ambulance moved away and the sergeant had finished with Leslie, who with an unlit pipe in his mouth, came back aboard.

"What did the police say?"

I watched her carefully. She was inquisitive but wanted at the same time for us to think that she was above that kind of thing if we weren't.

Leslie said that the sergeant didn't know anything. But there were no marks on the body so Leslie didn't think it could have been murder.

I knew Ella was going to say what she did about its being just like men not to be able to keep their eyes off a woman, especially if she had no clothes on, and I thought the words just suited her standing there as she was in her too-tight green cotton dress so that you could see the shape and strength of her thighs. And as she spoke it occurred to me that the line of wet clothes in the background was part of the picture too, of a coarse, sexually frustrated woman calling down the judgement of the Almighty on the sex she despised.

I had the impression at the time that she was talking to me more than Leslie, although it was to him that she spoke. She grudged me the glimpse I'd had of her. She said that we were evil bastards, both of us. Then she turned away.

Leslie winked at me. I noticed there were red specks in the whites of his eyes. He said she had got up the wrong side that morning. He nodded in her direction – she was sweeping near the stern – and he winked at me again.

But I remembered how through the wooden partition between the cabins it was her laughter which had wakened me that morning, and perhaps that was the beginning of it all and not the sight of her as she hung the clothes up. And I thought that perhaps she was angry with me because I knew about the eggs, because she had been caught out at a direct lie.

Leslie said he wondered what the hell was wrong now. I looked up and saw that the ambulance had halted at the other side of the vacant lot which ran directly on to the quayside. The driver was talking out of the window to a man in plain clothes. We watched without saying anything until the man stepped on the running board and the ambulance drove away.

"More to it than meets the eye," Leslie said.

I shrugged my shoulders.

I said it had nothing to do with us.

"We found the body, didn't we?"

"It might have been anybody."

"But it wasn't. It was us." He was reluctant to give up possession.

I didn't feel like arguing with him. I was thinking about Ella, wishing Leslie was to hell out of here so that I could make a play for her. I wanted her.

"Anyway," I said, turning away, "it's over now."

"Maybe," he said.

There wasn't much to do then until the lorries came with the load. We were leaving in the afternoon with a load of anthracite for Edinburgh and Leith. Ours was a motor barge, so we could move straight from the river to the canal without waiting for a tow. Both of us felt a bit uncomfortable there on deck and doing nothing because Ella never seemed to stop working. She had finished sweeping and now she was doing some vegetables in a wooden bucket. An occasional plopping sound came from it as the potatoes, peeled, white, and shining were dropped in.

She was sitting just that distance away so that you didn't know whether she could hear what you were saying or not, and every time I looked over at her I had the impression that she had just looked away, but maybe that was only imagination. It could have been, because since I had watched her stretch up to put the clothes on the line I couldn't get her out of my mind and I had a faint nausea at the pit of my stomach when I thought she might be aware of me as I was of her. I felt idle then for the first time in a long time because I felt she was watching me. Leslie felt the same thing for obvious reasons ("Are you going to stand there all day airin' yoursel'?" she would scream) and he was anxious to be occupied at some job or other, but evidently he could think of nothing to do. Ella, meanwhile, didn't appear to care whether we were doing anything or not. She just squatted there on a small wooden stool, her big bare knees showing, peeling potatoes and humming to herself. I couldn't hear her humming, but I got the impression she was, and I could see by the corners of her mouth that she was smiling.

Leslie began to talk about the corpse. He said that in his opinion she might have fallen in. If somebody had pushed her, there would have been more marks on the body, wouldn't there? She would have struggled. I asked him how he explained the fact that she had only a short petticoat on, that the skin of her buttocks was grazed. He said that she might have been drunk.

He knocked out his pipe and repacked it from a nondescript waterproof pouch. Now that he had said it, I don't think it convinced even himself. I glanced round, sure that Ella was listening. She was smiling at the potato in her hands. I watched it drop like a plummet into the bucket. She took another potato from the sack beside her.

Leslie asked me what I thought. He asked me if I thought she might have made a night of it. He meant, was she a tart who went aboard with some ship's officer or other? He was trying to visualize her drunk on deck with her skirt above her knees and her thighs splayed out for a man who later got rid of her.

I said: "She might have been pregnant."

But he said: "Naw, we'd've noticed."

His blue eyes were worried and his eyebrows were twisted in concentration and his pink sugarloaf head tilted backwards as though he were in pain. I was thinking about the slow white thing which sagged beneath the surface of the water and of the water-logged petticoat like the petal of a flower peeling back over the creamy weight of the thighs. The police-court details, the irrelevant series of after-images of the morning, the cat, the policeman with his mouth open, the parsnip-like appearance of the leg when the ambulance man tripped, the plain-clothes man who stepped on the running board, all that, and even the sudden coldness at my fingertips as I grasped at the ankle, had nothing to do with it.

It was strange, but Ella, on the contrary, was very close to it all, though she, strictly speaking, didn't come until later, close enough so that I could not think of the corpse without thinking of her. I can remember at that moment thinking how full Ella's lips were and how sometimes when she was cooking in the cabin little pin-heads of sweat stood out on her upper lip and when the light struck them they glinted.

Another image came back to me then. That was the day Jim spilled a cup of tea on the front of his mother's dress. She stood up with a squeal of rage, and there, three feet away from my eyes, I saw the heavy bulging outline of her lower belly, a flesh-colour through and sucked by the now transparent cotton which she hastily gathered up like a towel in front of her until she had stumbled through into my cabin from where she called angrily for her blue serge skirt. It had struck me as a joke at the time, perhaps because Leslie said that that was as hot as she would ever be in that place.

For a moment, when Leslie spoke next, I thought he was talking about Ella, for he said: "She was a bit heavy."

"Who?"

"The stiff!" He winked again.

"The water did that," I said.

"You think so?"

I lit a cigarette. Leslie and Ella, it was a strange combination. He must have been twenty years older than she. And with only a wooden partition between them and me I knew quite a lot about them. I knew for example that Leslie was impotent. And one night when he was drunk I heard them fight. They swore quietly at the other side of the partition, and then I heard them crash into the table. There came the sound of flesh smacking against wood, the scared voice of the kid, and then a dull thwack followed by a wild scream from Ella. He was thrashing her with his leather belt, sprawled face-downwards across the table. At least that's how I, without seeing it, saw it. After a while he left off. I heard him speak gruffly to the kid. Ella didn't make a sound.

"What do you really think, Joe?" he asked.

I laughed. I began to tell him a story about a bridge at night, and as I spoke I became conscious of the fact that I had raised my voice. I realised then that I wanted Ella to hear what I was saying. I told him that the woman had gone to the bridge fully dressed, and then, very calmly, she had undressed herself and dropped down into the water like a rose.

Leslie was looking puzzled. He didn't know whether or not I was trying to pull his leg. He asked me guardedly what kind of woman that was.

"Just an ordinary woman," I said.

"Some woman!" Leslie said, glancing unconsciously towards his wife.

I told him he might call her an exhibitionist. He asked me what I meant by that. He was suspicious. He didn't want to appear slow and I could see he was getting ready to laugh at a joke which was at present beyond him. He had taken his pipe from his mouth.

I glanced over at Ella. She was looking down into the wooden tub but I could see that she had stopped peeling the potato.

I said that she wasn't the kind of woman who could have committed suicide with her clothes on.

When I looked over at Ella again she was dropping the potato back into the bucket. It made a little splash. She found another one and began to peel it.

2

NOT LONG AFTERWARDS the lorries arrived with the anthracite. There were four of them and they backed up to the edge of the quay in turn and the load was shovelled down a metal chute straight into the hold. An open-deck scow would have been more practical but Leslie had to take what loads he could get. It was a dirty job for Leslie and me. After each load of anthracite had been emptied into the hold, he and I had to get to work with shovels and spread it evenly to prevent the barge listing. It wouldn't have been so bad working at the other end, but all the dust and grit in the world was down there in the hold and it got into our eyes and our noses and into the orifices of our ears. I never liked carrying coal or anthracite. The dust in my nostrils gave me a headache and it wasn't as though we could take a bath afterwards. We had to do it all in a wooden tub on deck and the water was cold with only a kettle of hot water poured in to take the chill off.

The loading took us about an hour and a half. I was hot and sticky and I could feel the coal-dust prickle on my skin under my shirt and when, in some context or other, Leslie mentioned Ella's name, I became vaguely and physically excited to imagine her against me, clean and warm and firm. I wondered how she would take it, whether her naked body would quiver and draw away or whether it would meet me with its own urgent thrust. I tried to imagine her with no clothes on, but in the constant movement of the anthracite and the rising dust I could not get beyond a vague white blur.

When we climbed out into the thin sunlight Leslie signed the receipt to say that he had taken delivery and the men drove away in the last lorry. We closed the hatch over the anthracite and then all we had to do was to sweep away the dust from the deck and get washed.

As we were in rather a public place – it was at the quayside on the Clyde in Glasgow, and we would go along the canal that joins the Clyde and the Forth, and then we would come back again with another load, whatever we could pick up in Edinburgh or Leith – we could only strip to the waist, and this was annoying because I could feel the coal-dust in my boots and on my legs and thighs. We could only roll up our trouser legs and stand knee-deep in the buckets. Ella had gone down below to get the kettle of hot water and Leslie and I relaxed on top of the hatch while we were waiting. I was no longer bored. From the moment I had wakened that morning things had begun to happen, nothing spectacular – I'm not talking about the corpse – but a kind of excitement at the edges of me. I was aware of a kind of prenatal odour in things. As I rolled my cigarette I could feel the dull ringing at the tips of my fingers, brought on no doubt by handling the shovel. The air smelled good. I wanted Ella to hurry up with the water.

Leslie, as usual, smoked his pipe. It struck me as natural that Leslie should smoke a pipe. He had big, heavy workman's hands with short broad fingers and he wore a gold signet ring on his left hand. His nails were short, cracked, and bitten to the quick, and the coal dust had settled on them, making them look grey and pink. My own were the same, only I didn't wear a ring and my fingers were a bit longer and not quite so rough. As I looked at the palm of my hand, moist and pink and grey, it occurred to me that if I placed my hand on a sheet of paper and pressed it there it would leave a clear and perfect impression. The mere thought of having my fingerprints taken made me feel guilty and I found myself wondering how a man could destroy all traces from a place where he had been. Leslie interrupted me to say that we would leave for the canal as soon as we had eaten.

I asked him where we would stop for the night. Night, since I had become aware of Ella, was full of possibility, especially if there was a pub close by to which Leslie would undoubtedly go. Apart from the existence of a pub, where we stopped for the night didn't matter. There was not much to pick and choose between the small towns along the canal. A few lights after ten o'clock at night, and they all went to bed early.

He said he didn't know, that all depended on how far we got before dark. He said we were in no hurry, that we had a load of granite chips to pick up in Leith on Saturday morning. It was only Tuesday.

The kettle of water arrived.

Jim came up from below with his mother and stood, eating another apple, staring at us.

"That boy eats too much fruit. He'll get the bellyache," Leslie said gruffly.

"Leave the boy alone," Ella said, carrying two buckets over to us. "You give me the bellyache with your complaints!" The buckets were both about half-full of cold water. Ella poured half the kettle of boiling water into each bucket, or roughly half, because I thought she was more Liberal with me.

"Hey, don't give him all the hot water!" Leslie said.

"Aw, shut your mouth! You're like a big kid!" Ella replied.

I liked the way she stooped to pour the hot water in, stirring it with her hand. I noticed there was damp patch under her arm and that the green cotton was discoloured there, a gradually paling yellow like a leaf in autumn.

We both stripped to the waist and began to soap our chests and arms while Ella went down below again to prepare the meal.

In spite of his age Leslie still had a big chest, but it rippled on to his paunch without clear definition. It struck me then that he must have weighed well over two hundred pounds.

He was snorting into the bucket, washing behind his neck, behind his ears, which stood out like little red lamps on either side of his head, shiny and tufted with small sprouts of grey hair. As far as I could see he was tattooed all over, with serpents and monograms and wreaths and hearts and anchors in green, blue and red inks. He'd got them done while he was still at sea. Each tattoo, he said, represented one woman, and he was able to bring back to mind their breasts, their thighs, their buttocks, the way they cried out – like alley-cats, most of them, he said, drawing extravagantly from his mean imagination – just by looking at the tattoos. Of course, he didn't get tattooed for every tart he slept with, just if they were special. Most of them weren't worth it.

Leslie met Ella in a seamen's canteen where she went to look for her father. Leslie was drinking with him in the lavatory because there were no drinks served there officially. They were both drunk and her father insisted that they should take Leslie home with them. Leslie had been ten years at sea as a stoker. Ella's father died shortly after they got married and Leslie gave up the sea and took to working the barge which Ella inherited.

When we had finished washing our fronts we washed each other's backs, dried ourselves and put on clean shirts. After that, we rolled up our trouser legs and washed our feet and legs and the kid was still standing there gaping at us and Leslie told him to beat it down below and tell his mother we'd be down in a minute. I was looking forward to going down myself. When the kid had gone he said we'd tie up at Lairs for the night. He knew a good little pub there where we'd be able to have a game of darts.

If there was anything Leslie prided himself on it was his darts. He played very well with a gentle little overhand movement surprising in a person of his weight and size. I can see him now, poised on the ball of his right foot, his tongue protruding slightly

34

between his lips, balancing one of his expensive metal darts on the tip of his short stubby fingers.

But I wasn't really interested.

Darts bored me just as much as Leslie's conversation. I was interested only in his wife.

After we had emptied the buckets over the side we went down to the meal. It was a good smell. She had made some soup and we were going to have some mince and potatoes afterwards. Jim was banging on the table with his spoon and his father told him to be quiet and behave himself. I was watching Ella ladle the soup into the plates. The pot was steaming. Beside it were two other pots. I could distinguish the bubbling sound of the potatoes and the stewing sound of the mince. I was hungry. She served the boy first and then she served Leslie and me and Leslie passed the bread which she had cut into hunks and we both dipped it deeply in our soup as we ate. A moment later she came to the table and sat down. Leslie and I sat one at either end of the table and she sat between us at the side opposite the boy. She rested her left arm on the table while she used the spoon.

All through the meal I couldn't keep my eyes off her. She had come to me suddenly, a woman hanging out washing with a vacant lot and a factory chimney in the background: it was as though someone had poured warm water on the back of my neck and it ran down over my front and back and down the inside of my thighs and down my legs and ankles. But the sensation didn't fade and leave me cold as the water would have. It lingered on my skin, reminding me of her. I couldn't keep my eyes off her and even when I looked down to dip the bread in the soup I was still aware of her.

She was close. Every movement, even the one I'd associated in the past with Leslie's wife during the three months I'd been with them, seemed to have taken on the same quality. It didn't matter whether she was reaching out for the bread and showing the yellow patch under her arm or standing at the stove serving the mince with the apron string lying loosely across her haunches or pushing back her straight short two-coloured hair which I'd never seen her brush, it had the same effect upon me. And I couldn't keep my eyes off her neck, which was the yellow colour necks sometimes are, and I couldn't help associating that with the change in colour of a stalk of grass of which the blade is green and dry relatively and then lower down, where the grass enters the earth, the stalk has a sweet milky appearance. It is smooth yellow-white, like ivory, only it has the smear of life, of what breeds. And if you compare a woman to a stalk of grass then her neck is the point at which she enters the earth, at which the sun strikes only intermittently, and below her neck she thrusts downwards, kinetic, towards the earth's centre, like the moist white shoots and roots of plants. I had often thought that. That was why I couldn't keep my eyes off her neck. And while I was eating my soup that was what I was thinking.

She got up to serve the mince.

As she did so the cotton of her dress fell softly about her thigh and it was as much as I could do to prohibit the impulse to touch her.

We didn't talk much at dinner. She scolded the boy once or twice for making a mess on the tablecloth and she asked Leslie when he intended to cast off. He said he wanted to get away as soon as the meal was over, and that irritated me because I like half an hour to digest my food. It was all right for him; his boat, his profits. But my irritation was only in the background, like a stray thought you don't take any notice of, because I was by this time too completely interested in Ella to pay much attention to what Leslie was saying.

When the mince came Leslie said to her what he had said to me about wanting to make Lairs that night. She said drily that it didn't matter to her where he got drunk. Leslie said defensively that I had challenged him to a game of darts.

Ella raised one eyebrow.

"Do you play darts?" she said, unconvinced.

I really didn't know what to say, for it was one of those questions spoken in that tone of voice which makes you feel very small and tongue-tied and to which, if the question is unexpected as this one was, you give a false, weak defensive answer.

"Sometimes, to pass the time," I replied.

"I thought you'd find something better to do with your time," she said more drily than ever.

I can't remember what it was I said then, but it was something that made Leslie laugh.

Ella got up and went over to the stove. Meanwhile, Jim was wondering what his father was laughing at and he asked his mother, who told him not to be inquisitive and to hold his tongue. "Eat your potato," she said, and to Leslie: "Don't rupture yourself!"

Leslie finished what was on his plate and a moment later pushed it away from him. By that time, with the feeling that I had said the wrong thing, I was finished myself and was going over in my mind the situation of a moment before in which, even allowing for the bias of my mind, I felt I had missed a cue, an opportunity anyway of letting her know that I knew the implication of her acceptance as natural of the fact that Leslie liked darts and the implication behind her sarcasm when she asked me if I liked darts too. Perhaps she was defending herself even then, against a fear in herself, when she placed me precisely and adroitly in the position of having to answer an awkward question. And her sustained sarcasm during the last few minutes, though it was not unusual at mealtimes when we were all congregated together, was aggravating now because since a few hours ago I wanted to change sides, to laugh with her at Leslie and not with Leslie at her. And so when she asked us if we would like a cup of tea and I saw that Leslie was getting ready to say no, that we would have to get under way and there wasn't time,

I said I would. "What about you, Leslie?" – and as I had said yes he shrugged his shoulders and said yes too.

I could see she was wondering why I had said yes so quickly and maybe she was amused. She had got that queer look on her face, a flush at her prominent, almost Mongolian cheekbones, which I had noticed before in the morning when she turned round from hanging up the clothes while the ambulance men were taking the body away and saw that I had been watching her. While she was brewing the tea she was smiling and humming to herself like she was when she was listening to my version of how the woman came to be in the water. I guessed that she knew I was interested in her.

She brought the cups over and put them on the table and then went back for the teapot and sat down in her place again.

I was rolling a cigarette and trying to appear casual, but inside I was alert and wondering just how far I could go. Leslie was reading the morning paper with a look of pained disbelief on his face and the nipper had a comic strip in front of him and was swinging his legs, as kids do, under the table.

That, and the fact we were walled into privacy by two newspapers, was what gave me the idea.

Of course, I was taking a risk and I might have been wrong about everything I thought had gone before, but even then I did not think she was likely to give me away. She was a woman after all, a woman who had been brought up on the barges. I watched a frail spout of steam issue from the kettle on the hob.

Slowly, very slowly, I moved my leg until it was touching hers under the table, until my shin was round under the back of her calf, and then, touching, I drew up my trouser leg to expose my shin and moved it softly up and down against the back of her calf. Her flesh was warm, the skin slightly rough. I had time to be conscious of that. I watched the flush spread from her neck to her cheeks, saw her stiffen, felt her whole torso quiver as, in collusion, she pretended not to know anything about it, and for a moment we sat in a kind of state of esoteric transmission, her profile towards me, her chin raised slightly, baring the thick sensuous line of her neck, her nostrils tense like shells and her right hand on the table gripping the salt cellar, playing with it. I spent the next minute consolidating my position, massaging gently with my shin on her bare flesh. Beyond, the newspapers rustled, Leslie coughed, and the kettle began to sing more energetically on the hob.

With a kind of eager reluctance then, I moved my hand on to her right thigh under the cotton. It was warm, soft, and elastic. She was breathing more heavily. She did not dare to look at me. Gently I stroked her, aware of the growing urgency at my fingertips as they sowed desire there at her thighs, an urgency which stemmed from the fact of my knowledge that my present advances could come to nothing, that at any moment the tension might be broken by the unconscious movement of one of the possible spectators. At that moment my fingers came into contact with the prohibiting elastic of her old-fashioned knickers. The balls of my fingers scored into her flesh, pushing their way under the elastic. At the same time I felt her downwards movement, incredibly slow and incredibly heavy, as she slid forward on the wooden chair so that her body raised itself almost imperceptibly to my fingertips.

At that moment she looked at me. It was almost, I felt, a look of hatred, her eyes brittle and passionate at the same time. I felt a fool suddenly to be watching her, to be at such a distance from her. I am sure she felt it too, but from her point of view it was a kind of treason. I tried to reassure her by glancing meaningfully over at the double bunk where Leslie and she slept. But that had the opposite effect from the one I anticipated. She breathed outwards quickly through tightened nostrils and heaved backwards with her rump to be free of my exploring fingers, at the same time moving her leg forwards away from mine in a delayed reflex action. Her left hand grasped with strong fingers at my wrist and thrust my hand from her. In her alarmed movement she must have kicked the kid for our private world was suddenly invaded by him: "Hey! Stop kickin' me, Ma!" and she clasped her hands on the table just as Leslie lowered the paper in front of him and said: "Well, Joe, if you've finished your tea we'll get started."

Ella was hot and confused and she was collecting the cups and telling the nipper to stop his yelling before she belted him. I stood up and said to Ella I'd enjoyed my tea very much, but she said something under her breath and didn't turn round. She was scraping the potato pot with a knife and I couldn't see her face.

3

U P ON DECK the air was cool, cool grey, and over behind the sheds the brick factory stack was enveloped in a stagnant mushroom of its own yellow smoke. Leslie spat out over the side of the barge and put away his pipe.

"I'll start her up, then," he said, and went below again.

I let go of the ropes and soon we had moved out into the yellow flank of the river into midstream and were heading for the entrance to the canal. The water was smooth and scum-laden and it seemed to lean against us and fall again, the surface broken with scum-spittles, as we made way. Now and again a piece of pockmarked cork moved past low in the water. There wasn't much traffic on the river. And then, under the dirty lens of sky, Leslie was looking intently towards the quay from which we had just pulled away, marking in his memory, I suppose, the stretch of water from which we had pulled the woman's corpse.

Now, it is boring when you get used to it to crawl along a canal, to wait for a lock to open, for water to level, but you see some interesting things too, like the cyclists on the footpaths where a canal runs through a town, and kids playing, and courting couples. You see a lot of them, especially after dusk, and in the quiet places. They are in the quiet places where there is no footpath and where they have had to climb a fence to get to. Perhaps it is the water that attracts them as much as the seclusion, and of course the danger. In summer they are as thick as midges, and you hear their laughter occasionally towards evening where the broken flowers spread down the bank and touch the water, trailing flowers. You seldom see them: just voices.

Of all the jobs I had been forced to do I think I liked being on the canal best. You are not tied up in one place then as you are if you take a job in town, and sometimes, if you can forget how ludicrously small the distances are, you get the impression that you are travelling. And there is something about travelling.

Soon we were chugging along the banks of the canal and it rolled away behind us like a very neat black tape dividing two masses of green-brown countryside. I could see a boom raised ahead in the distance. It looked very awkward perched there in mid-air like a sign that meant nothing but was black in the thin meagre afternoon light. I was at the wheel, which was aft, and Leslie was sitting on the hatch over the hold, smoking his pipe. He was gazing idly at the landscape, spitting occasionally, lighting and relighting his pipe. Ella was below, tidying up after the meal, and the kid was sitting up at the bows, cross-legged, looking from my point of view like one of those black things you see on telegraph poles. It was a peaceful sight. Leslie looked peaceful too, thinking no doubt how he was going to show off at the dartboard in the little pub at Lairs. I could see him raise a pint of beer to his lips, drink deep, leaving a layer of scum-coloured froth round the side of his glass. He would ask me then if I wanted a game of darts.

Yes, everything was peaceful, like the man who was ploughing in the field far over to the left and like the two cows which were grazing slightly ahead, and there was the fresh air all round me, and everything quiet and a little numb feeling of excitement somewhere deep down in me.

Standing there at the wheel, conscious of the pull Ella was exerting, almost as though she were hanging heavily and warmly from my skin, a heaviness which centred at the base of my spine and at the back of my thighs, and conscious at the same time of the flickering images of the afternoon, it came to me suddenly that touch was more important than sight.

Touch convinced in a way in which sight did not. I was struck by the fact that sight is hypnotised by the surfaces of things; more than that, it can know only surfaces, flatnesses at a distance, meagre depths at close range. But the wetness of water felt on the hand and on the wrist is more intimate and more convincing than its colour or even than any flat expanse of sea. The eye, I thought, could never get to the centre of things; there was no intimate connection between my eye and a plant on the windowsill or between my eye and the woman to whom I was about to make love.

And I remembered Cathie, whom I had lived with for two years before I ever came to the barge, and how sometimes I had looked at her and felt appalled by a sense of distance. Say she was sitting on the bed with her knees up, a book in her hands. Somehow, I was not convinced. She was there, but only indirectly, like the wallpaper or the cart drawing up in the street outside the window. I can remember as a small boy I loved touching things: trees, cats, flowers. I saw a violet or a rose but I had to destroy the distance, to feel the soft petals with my fingers, with my cheek; I had to draw the smell of it inside me and feel it living in myself. It was the same with Cathie. I had to go over and bury my head in her thighs – to feel her in my nostrils, to move my hand over her, and finally to draw her whole warm body close to me. But even that was not enough. Even touch was deficient. Perhaps she would be lying naked in my arms. I desired suddenly to see what it was that was so soft and moist and warm. Her body. But that was an abstraction, handy like a price-tag. It had nothing to do with the existence. I drew away from her and scrutinised her, the small breasts with their dull purple tips, the firm brown heap of her belly, and the resilient fleshiness of her thighs. Her buttocks were smooth and yellow, rounded like marble.

But I could not touch these things. I wanted to touch what I saw. But I could only touch a soft thing, a moist thing, a vibrant, clinging thing. Sight and touch may be correlative but their objects

43

are vitally different. Ceasing to see the rise of her breast as I pressed my lips to it to confirm it within myself, the thing which I wished to confirm fled away from me, and in its place was something soft and warm. There was no intimate and necessary relation between what I saw and what I touched. The impressions existed together like a stone and a melody, ludicrous, fraudulent, absurd. It is the feeling that something has eluded you.

I smiled when I thought of it. Cathie. I had met her for the first time in a holiday resort on the west coast. I had gone there because I had to get a job to earn some money. I was leaning on my elbows on the balustrade of the promenade, looking out across the sands towards the sea, I had been aware for some time of a slight movement, of the soft sea wind in coloured cloth, just below me on the beach. A girl was lying there, attempting with modest movements to oil her own back. I don't know whether at that moment she was aware of me. I allowed my eyes to fall occasionally and each time I did so she seemed to react by giving up the attempt to oil her back and by moving her oiled hand over the smooth flesh of her thighs and calves. They were well within her reach and she oiled them with great sensuality.

I watched for perhaps ten minutes. I felt sure by this time that she was inviting me to make contact with her and I was afraid that if I did not do so she would tire, gather her things together, and move along to a more populated part of the beach.

I walked quickly along to the nearest steps, descended to the beach, and walked towards her along the sand. I walked slowly, trying to gauge her reactions.

She was wearing sunglasses. Behind them, I felt her eyes focused on me, weighing me up.

There is a point at which a man and a woman stalk one another like animals. It is normally in most human situations a very civilised kind of stalking, each move on either side being capable of more than one interpretation. This is a defensive measure. One can, as it were, pretend up to the last moment not to be aware of the sexual construction that can be placed upon one's own movements; one is not bound to admit one's intention to seduce before one is certain that the seduction is consented to. But one can never be quite certain because the other is just as wary, just as unwilling to consent to a man who has not shown clearly his intentions are sexual as the man is to make his intentions obvious without prior consent. So a man and a woman fence with one another and the fencing is the more delicate because neither can wholly trust the other not to simulate ignorance of all that has passed between them. In every situation the man might be a puritan, the woman might wish to have the pleasure of being courted without the finality of the sexual act itself.

Cathie, for example, could have pretended, and, as a matter of fact did pretend, to be surprised at my sudden presence beside her on the beach. It had given her pleasure to be seen stroking her own limbs, but I had no way of knowing whether she would now consent to have me stroke them. She knew this, just as women usually know it, and she was going to enjoy having my purpose unfolded before her. At the point at which she was certain, she would be able to consent or not, and without reference to my desire.

I knew this and she knew it as I sat down beside her and offered her a cigarette. She accepted it. We talked casually about the weather, about the sun, and that made it possible for me to pick up the bottle of sun-tan oil and to examine it. She said I could use some if I wanted to.

I was still fully dressed and I had no bathing costume with me so I said there was not much point in it. Before she could interpret this as a withholding of myself I suggested that I could oil her back for her and I confessed that I had been watching her from the promenade above. She pretended not to know about this, but without a word she rolled over on to her belly and exposed her back to me. She was wearing a two-piece bathing costume of black nylon, the lower part sheathing her buttocks closely and the upper part hidden beneath her except for the thin strand of nylon which ran across her back just below her shoulder-blades.

I began at the small of her back, working with the oil in ever-increasing circles to the limits of her exposed flesh. Soon, however, the massage became a caress, and when I felt her succumb to it, her face buried in her towel in the sand, my fingers slipped first underneath the strap of the top half and then gently on to the smooth mould of her buttocks beneath the taut black nylon. She made no effort to resist. She had shut out the rest of the world from herself, shut out the fear of a casual onlooker from the promenade, by the simple expedient of closing her eyes.

Not far away were some rocks under which I knew it would be possible to be out of sight both from the beach and from the promenade. I did not even know the girl's name at the time and I was wondering whether it would be foolish to suggest going out of sight of other people. After all, even with my hands so intimately at work, she was presently quite safe, all fears gone and tensions relaxed. I could do nothing on the exposed part of the beach. And then, even if she were to consent, the sensations, the looseness which I had already caused in her might fade entirely as we moved to a more private place. She would have a hundred opportunities to revise and decide again. At that moment, had there been no danger of being witnessed, I believe I could have pulled her bathing costume down over her thighs, but whether, out of the sun, after a walk of a hundred yards, I would still be able to assert myself with a girl who was, after all a complete stranger, I couldn't know. The thought made me pause. I was unwilling to lose what I had already gained in a premature attempt to seduce her. But my doubts didn't remain for long. I felt her abandon. I saw she was totally oblivious

46

to the people who walked past on the promenade overhead. I leant down close to her and whispered that we could find a place to be alone together farther along the beach.

For a moment she didn't answer. She was lying with her eyes closed, so relaxed that she might have lost consciousness. I sensed then that she wanted to go wherever it was but that she had not yet overcome all her scruples. The longer she analysed, the cooler she would become. Follows, alas, as the night the day. And at such a point it is always difficult to know what to do.

I was a stranger. In the normal way of things there is a structure you have to build up of another person in terms of which that person must make his impact upon you. Beyond this structural idea there is no experience; the structure itself is armour against it. For two people to come close together it is necessary to destroy the structures in terms of which each experiences the other. Cathie had done just that when she accepted a stranger's caress. She could have no means of knowing what she was letting herself in for (unless it was the unknown). Cathie... that was the name of the girl on the beach. She had thrust away from her the whole system of weights and measures which a conventional upbringing had bequeathed to her. This she did tentatively – her back was towards me and she could at any moment turn, offended – but a tentative movement was all that was necessary. It is necessary only to act "as if" one's conventional categories were arbitrary for one to come gradually to know that they are, that the profoundest experiences are in the ordinary situation locked out from one's arena of experience by the inflexible barrier of good character.

As a stranger I was afraid of going too fast. As I say, in a situation like this it is always difficult to know what to do. If one is too quick a woman has her "suspicions" confirmed. She *knows* what you want but is able by some species of rationalization – and in spite of the fact that she knew all along what you wanted, knew, that is, that she had no need of confirmation – to be shocked by your proposal.

"I could do with a walk. Stretch my legs," she said at last, not looking at me. She got up. She added: "It's not far, is it?"

Perhaps she too was frightened her desire would be suffocated on the way.

"A hundred yards," I said, pointing, trying to appear more casual than I was. "Over by the rocks there."

Without another word she rose, lifted her towel and the small bag in which she carried her make-up, a book by Daphne du Maurier, and the other articles which a woman takes to the beach, and walked beside me in the direction of the rocks.

We walked separately, without speaking. When we had gone a few yards I took her bag from her and carried it for her. She allowed me to do this, and somehow the action and the consent, the smile, served as words would have.

The rocks were at the far end of the promenade, beyond the last hotel, and they rose up sharply and steeply enough to obscure anything on their seaboard side from the sight of whoever passed by on the promenade. They were shaped like a horse-shoe within which smaller clumps of rock rose upwards from the flat sand, forming tiny water-filled caves. We walked round the nearest point, which sloped down almost to the sea's edge, and as soon as we had done so we had the impression that we were in a kind of amphitheatre. Once inside, we followed the lee of the outer perimeter to a patch of dry sand, overhung by rock, but which was still in direct line of the sun.

I threw off my jacket, she arranged her towel, and we sat down. The inarticulate closeness which had existed between us a few moments before had evaporated. We were strangers again. She especially seemed suspicious and aloof. We smoked two cigarettes one after the other before she finally lay down and closed her eyes.

This time she was lying on her back, the disc of her belly gleaming with oil, her long legs apart and tapering downwards from the sleek casque of her bathing costume. Glistening particles of sand clung to her legs. There was no one in sight.

Cathie. But she was in the past, buried there deeply and finally. Now there was Ella.

But when she came on deck towards evening she didn't even look in my direction. She went forward to where Leslie was sitting and said something which I couldn't catch, and then she came back and I tried to hold her eye, but she avoided my glance and went below.

Her action disturbed me, the more so because I had been watching her and because even as lately as a few moments before when she was standing talking to Leslie the wind had lifted her skirt gently towards the stern and I could imagine what it would have been like if I had been sitting where the kid was and seen her from the other side. I thought then that the skirt would have been clinging up and against her left thigh, like a soft pew cloth in the wind, and that the muscles of her thigh would have been clearly outlined against the cotton. I found it difficult not to think speculatively about her body, to finger it in my imagination, and yet it had been there at the other side of the partition for two months.

Simultaneously, I derived a pleasing sense of detachment and isolation from the fact that she ignored me. It meant, after all, that she was aware of me, and from that I derived a powerful sense, a vindication of my own existence. To exercise power without exerting it, to be detached and powerful, to be there, silent and indestructible as gods, that is to be a god and why there are gods.

We would see the church tower of Lairs in the distance, a black cone against a red-flecked sky, a witch's hat in a haze of blood. It seemed very far away and enchanted.

Leslie said we would get there before seven. He knew a good place to tie up not far from the little pub he had told me about, so

49

we would have our evening meal and get along to the pub about eight. He wondered whether our discovery of the corpse would be reported in the evening paper. He hoped it would be. Anyway, he would see a paper at the pub. He was in high spirits.

The kid came back from the bows and went down below to his mother. Leslie took over the wheel and I sat down and had a smoke. I was thinking that I didn't want to go to the pub but I didn't see how I could get out of it. I didn't want to play darts, nor to drink for that matter, because Ella wouldn't have drunk anything and she might make that an excuse to refuse me, I had already decided to return earlier than Leslie.

Come to think of it, I had never been alone with Ella, not for more than five minutes at a stretch anyway, and we had hardly spoken. She had resented me from the first, perhaps because I was a man simply and because she judged all men in terms of her experience of Leslie. And of course during the first few weeks Leslie and I had grown quite close to one another. I was, I suppose, his ally against her. But now, after the dangerous intimacy at the cabin table, she must have known I was interested in her. I was anxious now to be alone with her so that I could see what her attitude was.

It was five to seven by Leslie's watch when we made Lairs. We tied up the barge in a little cutting off the main stream and before we went below he pointed out the road we would take to get to the pub afterwards. It was just up round the back of the church, he said, the cosiest little place I had ever seen.

Close up, the church tower looked just as disenchanted as most church towers in Scotland do. Later in the evening, as we skirted the churchyard to reach the pub, I noticed the usual ugly red and black posters proclaiming the evil influence of alcohol and the imminence of the Last Judgement.

"Let's go down and eat," I said. Leslie followed me.

The tea was already on the table, at least mine and his was, because Ella had had hers with the kid, Leslie grunted. He had no suspicions at that time.

It was sausages for tea, and bread and butter and jam to follow, so, as our sausages were already on the table, there was nothing for her to do except pour the tea. After she had done this, she sat down with her back to me near the stove and went on with her darning.

As I put mustard on my sausages I realized that now I was away from the wheel and the fresh air – the wheel itself under my hands had given me a sense of control – it was only natural that I should have lost that feeling of restrained tension which made me feel so good during the afternoon. It was not so easy down there in the cabin with their double bunk staring me in the face and her with her back turned towards me and Leslie so sure of himself he was thinking only of darts. To Leslie it must have seemed she wasn't thinking of anything. As though she was simply darning his socks, like she might have been shouting at him or scolding the nipper, and wondering how he got such big holes in them. But I knew she couldn't be as calm as she looked. She must have known she had let me go too far at the midday meal to expect me to have forgotten about it. I suspected that that was why she had had her tea early. She had probably thought it over during the afternoon and decided that no good could come of it, perhaps that I was getting ideas above my station, for I had known for a long time that Ella was a snob and she had set her heart on leaving the canal one day to go to live in a "nice little bungalow", as Leslie called it, in one of the quieter suburbs of Edinburgh. Whatever she was thinking, I decided that it was a good thing I was going to the pub after all, because a couple of whiskies would give me just the right amount of courage.

Leslie finished his food before me because he was anxious to get away to the pub. I have never known a man to hurry his meals so much. He gobbled, always, carrying gobbets of food to his mouth

ᴌ fork, not alternatively – it depended upon which
ᴌnt was nearest which piece of food and upon the shortest
ᴌnce between plate and mouth. He was leaning forwards now to
ᴌow the steam from the surface of his tea.

I looked at Ella's back. It was a broad back, the back of a woman who in maturity was beginning to spread, not slackly, for I could see that her flesh was still firm, but spreading nevertheless, so that a man might feel a powerful lust under him, opaque flesh, strongly muscled, and banded by the strong torque of her body's dynamism.

I intended to return to her, just as soon as possible. I was certain that beneath a few plausible inhibitions she felt as I did, hungry, as though there were a kind of elemental fitness between our respective lusts. I have always felt like that about sex. Each time I close with a woman I have the feeling that we were destined to come together, body to body, just on that way, at that time, in the field or in the bed or wherever it is, and I suppose that doesn't mean anything except that I am always there, waiting, ready to be caught up in it. I am like a sexual divining rod moving furtively at the edges of a meeting. I wait for a sign. It has something to do with the propulsion I feel from the instant desire is born in me, a shadow on a neck, the outline of a thigh, flanks, a gesture of lips wetting themselves, until the instant when I close with the woman. I resented Ella's present resistance. It was a kind of treason. She had already acquiesced. She could not back out. The whole thing sprang into existence when she stretched up to hang the clothes on the line, when the back of her thighs were bared momentarily up to perhaps six inches below her buttocks. And the risk we would run put an edge to it. I was certain that she was not unaware of my thoughts.

Leslie had already put on his cap and was waiting for me, so I went through into the small for'ard compartment where my bunk was to get mine. When I came back she was telling him not to get drunk. She had her back towards me and I winked at Leslie over her shoulder. Then I walked past her, brushing her buttocks with the back of my hand, and climbed up through the hatch. I felt her shudder. But she didn't say anything.

"See you later," I said without looking back.

I heard Leslie laugh from above as I climbed through.

4

A LITTLE BELL ABOVE THE DOOR tinkled as we went in.

It was a neat little pub with an open fire at one end and some bright brass ship's bells hanging from the rafters. An old man in a bowler leant across the counter and talked in a confidential voice to the barman, who wore a lick of hair, stranded and oiled, like a comb on his gleaming pink forehead.

The only other customer was a young man in a cap, who sat huddled over the fire as though he were trying to guard it against the room.

The barman nodded to us. He had prominent yellow eye teeth and pinkly blue bulbous eyes. The man in the bowler turned, nodded briefly, said how-do, and, resuming his confidential whisper, attempted to restrain the barman from hurrying to serve us. We waited politely a few yards along the bar.

Soon the barman approached us backwards, like a yoyo on a string, nodding all the time in response to the gradually expanding voice of the elderly man in the bowler hat.

"Scuse me, Mr Keith," he said suddenly, and turned to face us. "What'll you have, gentlemen?"

We ordered two whiskies and beers as chasers. When he had served us, the barman asked where we were from and Leslie told him we had come from Glasgow with a load of anthracite for Leith and the barman remembered him and asked him about another bargeman who used to come in sometimes – what was his name? – a small sallow man, he was, with a harelip and he always had a woman with him who looked like a gypsy, a girl of about twenty-five, an eye-catcher, but he hadn't seen him for months and he was probably dead or had given up the canal.

"Aye," Leslie said. "Like as not."

Leslie did not know who he meant anyway and Leslie knew pretty well all of the bargemen, so they concluded the man couldn't have been a regular.

The barman said discreetly that he wouldn't have minded having a go at the girl. She was anybody's meat, he said, not that he would have, being married and all with two fine children.

I was impatient. I didn't like the bar. I didn't like the barman's eyes, which looked as though they had been boiled in alcohol, and I had difficulty in pretending not to see the look of proffered friendship in the eyes of the old man who was now edging towards us along the bar. I saw nothing with attention. Time was passing, valuable minutes were passing during which I could have been alone with Ella or outside anyway and deciding how to go about being with her. I could not think clearly. Everything got in the way, the faces, the voices, the grease spot on the barman's tie, the hair on his pink arms, and his shiny yellow-white collar. I watched his Adam's apple move up and down as he spoke.

"How's business?" Leslie was saying.

I swallowed my whisky at a gulp and pushed my glass forward to be refilled.

The barman leant back, selected the bottle, and began to refill my glass. It was slack, he said. There wasn't any money about these days. Saturday wasn't bad.

"Same everywhere," Leslie said.

"Taxes," the voice of the man in the bowler hat said. The man in the bowler hat didn't look as though he had paid a tax in the last twenty years.

"Follow you to the grave," said the barman. "Costs you a pretty penny to die these days."

Leslie laughed.

"Talking of the dead," he said, "you don't by any chance have an evening paper?"

"Sure. What's up?"

Leslie explained that he and I had picked a stiff out of the river that morning. "She was stark naked," he said.

The barman whistled and the old man with the bowler took the cue to move up and join us.

"Murder?" he said. He had a long chin and his watery eyes were unpleasant. He was looking at me, inviting confirmation.

"Must've been," the barman said, "if she had no clothes on. Young?"

Leslie said that it was difficult to say, but that she couldn't have been more than thirty. He asked me what I thought.

I said: "She was twenty-seven."

"Was she cut up like?" the man in the bowler asked, screwing up his eyes.

"Not a mark," Leslie said untruthfully, for the buttocks had been rather badly scratched. "Here, have you got yon paper?"

The barman reached under the counter for it and passed it across to Leslie, who moved systematically over the columns with his thumb.

"Let's have another drink," I said.

The barman poured it automatically, changed the coin, and I retreated from the bar and sat with my drink at one of the tables. The conversation came to me from a distance. I examined the whisky in the glass, allowing it to ride against the sides as though I were searching for something in it. Of course I was. But my gaze was the kind of impotent gaze that a man in the gallery casts at a chorus girl in the front row. At that moment I resented my poverty, intellectual as well as economic.

Just then I heard Leslie say triumphantly: "There it is!"

"Where, for Christ's sake!" the barman said.

"There!"

"There. Bottom of the third column. Look!"

And he read:

The body of a dead woman was found in the River Clyde early this morning. The woman was wearing only a thin petticoat. She is so far unidentified. The police are investigating the possibility of foul play.

"Thought you said she was naked?"

"Same thing. These petticoats is transparent."

It was not difficult to leave before Leslie. I told him I had a headache. The man in the bowler had offered to play darts with him. I said good night all round and left.

In the fresh air it came to me that I'd had too much to drink, not really too much, but enough to slow down my reactions, to make me careless and know it without being able to do anything about it. I felt it in my walk and it worried me.

I walked slowly down the narrow road past the church and stopped to read the posters which I had glanced at on the way to the pub. It was too dark to see them. I found myself lighting a match and holding it close to the boards. The match burned my fingers and went out. I cursed silently and stepped backwards. Farther down the road, I said good night to a policeman who I felt sure was watching me. Then I crossed the road quickly and turned down the little side-street which led to the canal. I was already thinking about what I was going to say, but by the time I reached the canal and when I came within sight of the barge I stopped to blow my nose and laughed at myself for being nervous. I was nervous, without a single thought in my head about how I was going to do this thing, about how I was going to break in on Ella's world finally because I was set that way and had been since early morning. I listened to the fall on gravel of my own footsteps.

The barge was lumpish, in shadow as I walked towards it. Somewhere nearby a dog barked.

Now it was dark and the canal water was there as witness. It forced itself on me, a sound, a smell, present as we walked. She was walking at my side and I had my arm round her waist. Even at the time I was unsure how I had persuaded her to leave the barge with me.

It was a dark night on the towpath and there was no moon. Her face was there, just a bit phosphorescent beside me. I tried to recall the argument and how scared she had been that the kid would wake up, and then the sudden lift, her voice almost triumphant, when she agreed to come on deck with me. We were walking past a hoarding when she stopped. She said she wasn't going any farther, but she said it softly, as though she were afraid of being overheard. It was not that she was resisting me. Realizing it, I moved her against the hoarding and stood very close to her. It was a chill night. I had experienced before this conjunction, I mean the cold air containing the warm smell of a woman, warmer for the air's being cold. I realized suddenly that her clothes were not part of her. It sounds like a truism. But in the intensity of the moment it is a wonderful discovery. The cloth seemed to crumple beneath my hand, and I felt the strong flank muscles arching firmly beneath. I had to put my hand under her chin and tilt her face upwards towards me. And then I slipped my hand under her coat to her thigh. The cotton dress, the same one, was warmer under my fingers. I could feel that she wasn't wearing anything underneath. The dress lifted lightly over my wrist as I brushed my hand upwards over her skin. I kissed her then at the same time and we stood there swaying slightly as though the light night wind, smelling of the canal, had the power to move us.

She sank downwards on to the grass. I followed her. And then my hand feathered her strong belly, teasing the flesh towards the navel, where, abruptly, the belt of the dress girdled her, making her belly curve upwards like a great white moon of sensuality. She was breathing heavily, her heavy thighs widening to encourage pressure. She had closed her eyes. Her frock, peeled upwards now above her hips, revealed the derelict posture, from the abdomen downwards, the knees slightly raised, the whole creature part of her like a strange night animal trapped beyond its lair. I moved downwards. Across her belly, across the thigh that rose against my cheek, I saw the glimmer of the canal water, and beyond that nothing, for the houses on the opposite bank were already lightless, their inhabitants asleep. The dog barked in the distance.

It was perhaps the dog's bark that brought me back to time. I don't think I have ever seen anything lovelier than Ella in her abandoned position. The obstinate stupidity was gone. The futility of her existence was utterly transcended. I heard her say huskily: "Now, Joe," and a moment later we were together, fused, as lead is fused to lead, and the dew on the grass was on her and on the backs of my hands where they held her.

Later, she rose from the grass like an animal shaking itself into wakefulness, and I had lit a cigarette and was standing away smoking with my back against the hoarding. I noticed then for the first time that there were stars.

I watched her tidy herself. She did it impatiently, or rather with the air of impatience, because she moved slowly, as though she were giving herself time to compose her face before she looked at me. I watched her button up her coat.

"The police are investigating that woman," I said.

She looked at me. "What made you think of that?"

"Something to say."

"You've done enough talking for one night," she said.

I could not see the expression on her face.

"Are you sorry?"

"A fat lot of good that would do me!"

"We'd better be getting back," I said. "I told Leslie you'd have a cup of tea ready for him when he got back."

"You would!"

She was bending down, brushing her bare legs with her hand. As she rose again, I pulled her towards me and kissed her. For a moment we tried to see each other's eyes in the dark and then she freed herself.

"Get back to the barge," she said. "We must."

She made me walk apart from her and, as the towpath wasn't wide enough for two to walk abreast and apart at the same time, she walked in front.

As I followed, I was wondering what thoughts were running through her head, whether she regretted it now it was over or whether she would want to develop the relationship. I knew that Leslie wasn't much use to her in that way. She had told me her age: thirty-three. She was probably two years older. I wondered whether I was the first. I supposed I was. Living with him on the barge, it wouldn't be easy for her; they were moving most of the time. And anyway, she did not strike me as the kind of woman who would go out looking for it. She was a snob. And she despised men, at least up till now she had, or pretended to do so, with that thick sarcastic voice of hers, stupidly and obviously; but up till that time I had not thought of disbelieving her because even if she had only consciously formed a habit of despising them, it came to the same thing. In the end she would do so. But now I wasn't too sure.

We climbed on to the barge and went down below and put the light on. The kid was still sleeping. The paraffin lamp was smoking, scorching the globe, and she leant over the table to turn it down.

As the lamplight struck her face I noticed again how full her lips were. She was the kind of woman I liked, mature, strong-bodied, with a thick opaque quality of flesh. Her hair, though cut short, was quite straight. In spite of the fact that I hadn't been aware of her before, I found myself thinking that she was the kind of woman a man was bound to be conscious of, a woman whose body was still young, not fat, and yet which appeared at the belly, hips and breasts, to be about to tear through the fragile too-much-washed cotton dress which encased it. If she turned at the waist, it seemed, the cotton would rend apart.

"Too bad he's coming back," I said.

She finished with the lamp.

"What?"

"Too bad he's coming back."

I nodded towards the double bunk. There was something seductive about the heavily planked bunk with its faded quilt which was almost colourless in the soft yellow light of the paraffin lamp. Through the partition I had heard it creak under their weight often, and that time in the middle of the night I had heard the thick searing sound of the heavy leather belt; swearing, muffled conversation too, but the noises were always too spasmodic and infrequent for them to be those of a man and woman making love.

"In there," I said. "In the bunk."

She smiled at me for the first time since I had raised my body from hers.

"You're nice, Joe," she said, squeezing my wrist. And then she turned away and lit the gas under the kettle. I sat down at the table and glanced at the morning paper.

"Did you bring the paper back with you, Joe?"

"No, Leslie's got it."

"What did it say about that woman?"

"Not much. Just that the police were investigating."

She shrugged her shoulders and didn't say anything. I saw her profile from where I was sitting. Her face was set, heavy at the jaw, slightly sullen, tilted downwards, looking at the kettle as though she were willing it to boil. Behind, on the planks of the partition, was her shadow. I watched that for a moment and then returned to the paper. The kid was still asleep in the small bunk opposite the double one. When I looked up again the cat was rubbing itself against her ankles.

"Are you hungry?" she said. Her back was turned to me. Her voice came again. "I could fry you an egg."

It was a confession.

"Not now, Ella. Just a cup of tea."

A few moments later we heard footsteps on the towpath, and then the clump of Leslie's boots on deck.

"It's him," she said without looking round, just as Leslie, climbing downwards and backwards, descended into the cabin. Sometimes he did that, although the steps were broad enough for a person to come down the other way. I supposed he had been drinking heavily after I left.

When he turned round my first thought was that he knew about Ella and me. He looked at us, from one to the other, without speaking, and then he slipped off his raincoat and hung it up on a peg. He sat down at the table opposite me and looked at his folded hands on the table in front of him. The lamplight accentuated the scarred and dust-pitted surfaces of his stubby fingers.

"You two are bloody quiet," he said.

"Pity you aren't," Ella said without turning round.

I glanced at her. It was as though she had suddenly become herself again. She was putting on her apron. When I looked back at Leslie I saw that his face had changed too. He had that hurt, sullen expression on his face that a drunk man has when he is afraid of a woman and unable to answer her back. He looked out of the corner of his eye at me.

"What's up, Leslie?" I said.

"I know damn well what's up!" Ella said harshly, still without turning round. "He's been losing money at darts again. Then he comes back here and tries to take it out of me! Just you shut your damn mouth, Leslie Gault! You'll get no rise out of me!"

"I never lost a penny at darts!"

"You're a liar!"

He looked as though he was about to strike her, but evidently he thought better of it. He said instead, a cowed tone entering his voice: "Is the tea ready yet?"

"Wait your hurry! Do you expect to come back at this time of night and have us all at your beck and call?"

Leslie drooped. Ella's back was still towards us. Looking at her now I realized that you had to think in terms of two women, his and mine. His was hard. I could understand his dumb frustration, even sympathize with it. Mine he had probably never known. It was difficult to square what I supposed was his experience of her with the woman who, half an hour previously, had bared her belly for me against the boarding and then sunk downwards through my arms on the grass.

The cabin clock, a little brass clock nailed above their bunk, struck ten. Ella was now brewing the tea, and Leslie, apparently recovered from his loss of face, asked me what I thought of the mangy write-up of our discovery in the paper.

I said I wasn't really interested.

"They always catch them in the end," Leslie said.

I didn't reply.

Ella poured the tea. She had removed her apron again and I felt her leg close to mine under the table. I put my hand on her knee under her dress and let it lie there, just moving my fingers slightly. The flesh was warm and putty-like. She made no attempt to restrain me. But she didn't respond nor show in any way what was happening to her either. We sat like that, talking in a desultory way of nothing in particular for about half an hour, and then I turned in and left them together in the main cabin. I could hear their voices talking on for a while as I lay there in the bunk with the blanket drawn over me until the light in their cabin, which penetrated through the seam between two of the planks in the partition about a yard from where my feet were, was suddenly put out. After that I couldn't hear what they were saying and anyway wasn't interested. They were talking as husband and wife talk, and that had nothing to do with Ella and me and our coming together. Leslie was irrelevant. Presently he began to snore. It suddenly occurred to me that she might risk visiting me during the night, but I put the thought away from me again. She wouldn't do that. I lay awake for a while. I could still feel her skin against mine, like smooth rubber surfaces meeting, and I supposed she could still feel me, even though she was in a bunk with another man. In a sense she wasn't with Leslie at all but there with me all the time, in touch, in smell, in traces on my skin and in my nostrils as I fell asleep.

I closed my eyes. I listened to the lapping of the water against the side of the barge.

5

THE SLOW LICK OF THE WATER against the belly of the barge was still present when I awoke, as though during the night it had guarded the connection between states of waking and sleeping, the noise of the water only, for my cabin had changed under the pale log of light which entered at the port, defining clearly the greyness of the blanket, the chipped varnish of the plank walls which closed me in. Often when I woke up I had the feeling that I was in a coffin and each time that happened I recognized the falseness to fact of the thought a moment later, for one could never be visually aware of being enclosed on all sides by coffin walls. As soon as one saw the walls, as soon as light entered one would no longer be cut off and so the finality of the coffin would have disintegrated. And then I would be conscious again of the sound of the water and of the almost imperceptible movement of the barge in relation to it.

That morning I was awakened by the smell of cooking bacon and by Leslie coughing in the main cabin. Leslie always coughed in the morning. You would have thought he was coughing his insides out, a big rasping cough which began somewhere deep down in his chest and ended with a struggle in his throat, as though all the poisons in his body had collected in his lungs during the night.

The convulsion lasted about five minutes and then I heard him banging out the dottle in his pipe on the side of his bunk. A moment later he would have it filled again and he would be sucking the flickering match flame into the heavy sweet black tobacco.

I ate a square of chocolate and as I screwed up the wrapper the fact of Ella gradually dawned upon me again, a small needle-sharp excitement above and behind my loins. Ella. I was glad the day had arrived. Everything was changed, including my attitude towards the barge, towards the canal. For the first time for weeks, I was looking forward to getting out of bed.

Not long afterwards, Ella opened the door and came in with my morning cup of tea. She gave us both a cup of tea in bed every morning. Usually she came into my compartment, laid the cup on the orange box which served as a bedside table and went out again. Usually, if I bothered to look at her face, I saw hostility there, at least impatience. This morning it was different. I watched her hesitate in the doorway with the cup in her hand. Then, without speaking, she put the cup on the box but instead of going out immediately she dropped down on her knees beside the bunk and ran her hand under the blanket over my body and down the side of my flank. I tried to lay hands on her, but she evaded me with a laugh.

"Drink your tea," she said.

She waited until she saw me drinking it before she went out again, and then I heard her heavy walk on the wooden floor of the main cabin. I closed my eyes. Each time her feet moved, the impact of her foot on the floor would send a minute quiver up the sinews of her leg into the ambiguous and tensile mass of her broad thighs. I could almost smell her again. I felt suddenly relaxed.

I was standing on deck. I was looking along the canal bank, and there, about a hundred yards ahead, was the hoarding and the grass verge where we had lain down. About twenty yards behind the hoarding was a cottage of whose presence we had been unaware the previous night. We had made love almost in its garden.

"Nice little house," Leslie said.

I nodded.

We both looked at it for a moment and I wondered if the situation was as artificial for Leslie as it was for me. It was as though, because we had nothing to say to each other, we had tacitly agreed to feign interest in the same thing, for the cottage must have had different associations for him and for me, and it occurred to me that human beings often compromise with each other in this way, choosing what is apparently, but each knows certainly not to be, a point of contact, simply because to admit openly that no point of contact exists is to imply the superfluity of the other, and thus to undermine his very existence. And so we looked together at the same cottage and I said: "It needs reslating, though." And Leslie, catching the thread, a matter of unconscious habit for him perhaps, went on to say that reslating was expensive these days, and so the shuttle moved backwards and forwards between us, neither of us willing to interfere with the glib mechanism, not at least until an alternative point of contact suggested itself, and what we said was trivial but our saying of it was not. That was often the way between Leslie and me, and since the previous night the actual distance between us had increased immeasurably because I was aware of something which concerned him intimately and was unable to speak of it.

Conversation was difficult that morning. Leslie thought of something for us to do, I forget what exactly, with a hammer and nails, and Ella came on deck with her shopping basket while we were doing it. She watched for a few moments and then, without saying anything, she went along the canal bank and out of sight into the road leading up to the church. Leslie was more involved in the job than I was. As I bent down over the wood, I watched her walk away swinging the wicker basket by her side. I never get tired of watching women walk, especially if they walk as Ella did, with slow, heavy movements and a spring that did not come to the surface but vibrated at the thighs and at the haunches like a force held in check.

"Mind your thumb," Leslie said, "or I'll cut it off."

He was grinning at me and I found myself steadying a plank for him, and Leslie with a three-foot saw in his hands. That surprised me because I had not been conscious before either of the presence of the saw or of the new position I had taken up. I moved my hand slightly.

The moving saw began to retch its way into the wood.

"Think it'll rain?"

I looked up. The sky was beginning to be overcast, as though part of it were being stained gradually at its edges by the other part, while the sun, obscured now, was bright in reflection, quite cold, and appeared behind the darker part as a shatter in glass.

"Looks like it," I said.

"We'll go down and make a cup of tea," Leslie said. "There's nothing much to do anyway."

The canal was choppy at the surface.

We were drinking tea when Ella came back. She had been caught in the rain, soaked to the skin, she said, and she got behind me and changed her dress. Leslie was reading the morning paper which she had brought back with her, and presently he looked up from the paper and said: "Not a word about it here, Joe. An old woman's had her head bashed in in Paisley, but there's nothing about our one."

Behind me, I could hear Ella's movement and her breath seemingly caught up and let out again as she stepped into dry clothes, and there was a sliding sound, soft, prickling slightly, as they passed upwards over her legs and thighs. I was conscious of the smell flesh has when it has been close to garments soaked by the rain. I fought an impulse to turn round. Then her voice said:

"What's it to you anyway? Can't you leave her alone now she's dead?"

Leslie grunted inarticulately. When he spoke it was to say that the old woman had sat upright in her armchair for three days after she was dead and if the milkman had not noticed that her milk remained uncollected at the doorstep and reported it to the police she would still be there dead, with her head bashed in, in the empty house.

"Funny that," said Leslie brightly. "Sometimes you don't know what's under your own nose."

Lunch went much as usual. I touched Ella once under the table. She flushed faintly and went on eating. The kid talked incessantly but none of us was interested in what he was saying. When we went on deck, the rain was off, but over the fields and the canal gusts of whiteness blew, not rain, but damply wild, visible only when they thickened under the force of the wind, making the atmosphere bracing and uncertain.

As I stood at the wheel and we moved slowly along the canal, that uncertainty communicated itself to me, making me impatient to be with Ella again, and I wondered what she was doing, thinking, if she was waiting down there below, also fidgeting and impatient. I imagined the warmth of the cabin, the wood, the leather, the stove. Had I been alone on the barge with Ella, I would have tied up to the bank. In the cabin we would have been aware of the weather but untouched by it. The barge would have rocked gently as she climbed naked on to the bunk for me.

Later in the afternoon, Ella came on deck to hang up some wet dish towels. She did this near the stern where the wheel was and I had an opportunity to speak to her, but she was evasive, pretending in the wind not to catch what I said, and when she had hung up the towels she went below again. I had the impression that she was slipping away from me. Leslie went below then. About ten minutes later, he came back on deck with a cup of tea for me. He took the wheel while I drank and my eyes returned to the landscape where, whitely, in gusts, the trees and fields were swept as though by invisible brushes.

As evening approached, Clowes came in sight: another small canal town, more industrial than Lairs.

We noticed the fair immediately. The marquees were pitched in the fields to the left which bordered the canal, and the hurdy-gurdy music was suspended in the atmosphere for a long time before we saw them, or the stalls or the brightly painted caravans and lorries. Jim was up at the bows in his usual place, only now he was excited and gesticulating frantically and soon Leslie went forward to him and they spoke and then Leslie lifted the kid on his shoulders so that he could see better what was there. Ella too came up from below, looking questioningly up round the hatch. She had heard the music.

I realized then that the fields were out of the question that night, even supposing I succeeded in getting Leslie away from the barge and got back myself. I felt Ella look at me and look away. She was finding fault with me, I felt. Ever since she had come on deck to hang the towels up, the feeling that she was sliding away from me had persisted like a toothache all afternoon, and now her glance and the way in which she turned away again without a sign and without speaking confirmed my doubt. I almost called out to her, but when she disappeared below again I was glad that I hadn't because I would not have known what to say. Leslie came back along the deck towards me.

"See it?" he said, nodding backwards over his shoulder. I nodded.

Leslie sat down beside me and we both looked and listened. Then, on the towpath not far ahead, we saw a man. He was sitting on the grass verge, leaning forwards, his shoulders hunched, his chin on his chest. As we approached him he did not look up.

"Tramp," Leslie said.

"Not much of him."

Leslie glanced at me.

"The tramp," I said. "Look at his boots."

Two white sticks, the shins unsocked, like a thin neck from a collar, thrust upwards from split boots. The man's head under the old fedora remained tilted upwards as we passed.

"Can't hear us," Leslie said.

"He's not interested."

Leslie tapped out his pipe on the deck.

"Scare the birds," he said.

"Poor bugger."

"A man won't work," Leslie said.

"Not much work left there," I said.

"For the crows," Leslie said.

"Or the rain, Leslie."

"You'd be surprised," Leslie said. "A few nights in the open. They get toughened to it."

And we both looked backwards but the man hadn't moved. He was folded like a penknife at the waist as though for the last time.

"Might be dead just sitting there."

Leslie laughed incredulously.

"You never saw a dead tramp," he said. "They don't die like the rest of us."

"Who buries them?"

"A pauper's grave," Leslie said. "But they don't die in the open. They go indoors to die."

The music from the fairground was louder now and we could see the brass poles of the roundabouts spiralling upwards and downwards, faintly flashing gold.

"Not much farther," Leslie said. "We'll tie up along there." He indicated with his pipe: "See, just beyond those trees."

"Do you think he was dying?"

"Who?"

"The tramp."

"Drunk more likely. Might take a look at the fair tonight, Joe... what d'you say?"

"Sure," I said, "it might be interesting."

Leslie was looking back again.

73

"There he goes," he said. "Jesus, just look at that, will you?"

The tramp had shifted. Still bent, the crumpled trousers tight on his shanks, he was moving off in the opposite direction, more like a windmill than a man.

We tied up a few minutes later. And then Ella was calling on us to come down for our tea. The kid had had his hair brushed. It was wet round the edges and stood up like stalks on his flat head.

"You can think of your son for once and take him over to the fair for a while after," Ella said.

"What about you?"

"I've got work to do. You take the boy."

Ella hadn't looked at me since I had come down, but the thought hadn't occurred to me until she spoke because I had been thinking almost exclusively about the tramp and wondering whom he reminded me of.

It wasn't a direct resemblance, but there was a connection somewhere with someone. Something vaguely familiar. I wasn't able to put my finger on it until later. The familiarity was the familiarity of limbs out of control, of something missing that should have been there, the absence of which, more telling than what remains, strikes at one deeply, almost personally, making one feel that one is face to face with the subhuman. The dead are like that, and the maimed, and the tramp was. As he moved off in the opposite direction, a triangle of white afternoon light dangled between the raking black legs, the hoop of his back supported arms twisted horizontally, like a tuberous root above them, and the head, a knob under the hat brim, looked in no direction as though direction were irrelevant now, and the canal and time and the barge which had passed him while he sat folded up on the grass verge were irrelevant too, all except the gratuitous movement in which he was involved and which was not his own because somehow the man was absent from it. He had come close then to my memory of the corpse in the water, which was only a movement of limbs, less rigid than his but in some unmistakable way the same.

When Ella spoke, I gave up trying to find the connection. When I looked at her she had raised the cup to her lips and they were touching the surface of the tea tentatively, pushing away and sucking at the same time. She was looking straight in front of her.

"I'll stay aboard if you'd like to go," I said easily.

I knew she was going to refuse but I wanted to remind her I was there, in case she had forgotten; but somehow I was afraid to touch her under the table. There was a wall between us, inexplicably there suddenly. Her passion for me had evidently, unaccountably, staled.

"I've no time," she said. "You can go too."

"OK. We'll go," Leslie said enthusiastically, and conscious perhaps that my enthusiasm didn't match his, he added: "We don't need to stay too long, Joe. Just stretch our legs."

"Sure," I said. And it occurred to me that this way Ella would be alone on the barge.

The ring of coloured lights was turning. A man was speaking through a megaphone. The stalls opened like bright yellow mouths laughing. The hurdy-gurdy music formed a ceiling over the jutting squares of electric light bulbs. The timbers of the switchback were high over on the left. Leslie led the way, pushing through the crowd, turned, grinned back at me over Jim's head and then moved on through the crowd.

Then at one stall the penny rolled down the chute and landed on a square marked "4d". The woman tossed four pennies flatly across the squared cloth. Leslie retrieved them.

"Always win," he said.

Above, above everything, the night was dark blue. The board at the upper rim of the stall read "Abbott Bros". It was scored with mud and paint. A man on my left was pressing against me, a weight of shoulder, smelling of brilliantine and tobacco. Leslie had lost. His last penny landed on the dividing line between two numbers. He was calling for change. The moon face of the woman with crinkling blonde hair seemed to swim across the stall at me. The man beside her, a thin little man with a pencil-thin, black moustache, in shirtsleeves and a greasy black soft hat, was looking at a roundabout: her husband.

"Fivepence," Leslie said, pointing.

It was raining. I had been aware of it for the last few minutes.

"Sorry! Just touching the line as you can well see! Coins must not touch the line!"

"It's raining, Les."

"Bloody highway robber," Leslie muttered. He saw now that none of his coins had landed properly.

"I've still got fourpence," Jim said.

The shoulder dunted me. "Excuse me," it said.

"It's raining, Les."

Somebody was making a commotion at the back of the crowd. I leant forward under the roof of the stall to be out of the rain which spat coldly in. I was thinking of Ella. Jim had won three-pence. The pennies came back to him. Clunk, clunk, clunk. The roundabout had stopped. People, turning up collars, were dismounting hurriedly.

"It's raining, Les."

"What?"

"Rain," I said, exposing it like a magician in the palm of my hand.

At that moment the commotion touched my shoulder. I turned round. A black face and white teeth, one gold one, was smiling. "Sorry, you with him?" Pointing over my shoulder. "Leslie!"

Leslie turned.

"Bob! Bob Mabuski! What the hell are you doing here!"

They shook hands over Jim's head.

"I quit. I'm living here now," Mabuski said.

The rain was getting heavier.

"Won't last," someone was saying.

"I've got sevenpence," Jim said.

"On the canal. We move off tomorrow morning," Leslie was saying.

People were hurrying away under umbrellas. A crush of three rushed past under one mackintosh.

"Come somewhere where it's dry."

His friend, Mabuski, led the way. We reached shelter under the tall skeleton of the switchback. Leslie introduced me to Bob. They had worked for the same company though they had never served on the same ship. They reminisced about some eastern port, Miki or Kiki, a coaling port where every house was a brothel. After a few minutes the fairground was deserted except for people who had preferred to take shelter here and there amongst the stalls. The rain became heavier still, forming quick puddles on the grass. The music had been turned off. We listened to the noise of the rain.

"It can't last," Leslie said.

Jim was despondent.

"Never mind, son, we'll come back another time."

"I don't want to go back yet," Jim whimpered.

"How's the wife, Leslie?" Mabuski said.

The wetness rose damply with its smell and the smell of the grass and circulated round our trouser legs.

"Fine, Bob. How's yours?"

"She's expecting."

"Ha!"

"We're looking for a house. Got a flat but it won't be big enough now with the kid."

"Sure," Leslie said. He stared into the curtain of rain. "We'll make a dash for it in a minute. Would they let the nipper into a pub?"

Bob shook his head. In the dim light his hair had a grisly appearance and the raindrops moved downwards slowly from his temples to his cheeks. Walls with rain on them, I felt for a moment.

"Where could we go then?"

Bob shook his head again. "I'd ask you to my place but the missus is in bed. She's resting."

"I don't want to go home," Jim said.

"Hell, what a night!" Leslie said.

"You could take him to the pictures," Bob said. "There's two of them in town."

"Would you like to go to the pictures?"

Jim said yes, that he didn't want to go home. Leslie asked me if I would go along. The lights of the roundabout were switched off suddenly, and it stood there, off at a distance, cornet-shaped, ghostly, still. A voice said: "Where's that bloody tarpaulin?" Evidently they had decided to close down for the night.

"Better get going soon," Leslie said. "What d'you think, Joe? You come along?"

"To the cinema?"

"Aye."

"No thanks," I said. I lit a cigarette, shielding the match in my hands. The palms, close to my eyes, were the same palms which would raise Ella's body, causing her to fall apart like an open book pressed upwards at the spine. That gave me a strange feeling. The match went out and I lowered my hands.

"What'll you do then?"

Did he suspect? I didn't think so.

"Don't worry about me," I said. "I'll walk you into town, have one drink with you and get back to the barge. I've got a good book."

The rain was slackening, going off, very suddenly, as though some weatherman in the sky had turned off a tap.

"Don't know how you can read them things," Leslie grunted.

"Come on now," Bob said. "It might come on again. We'll make a run for it."

We moved out from under the switchback. Everything was dripping, ropes, beams, trees, and the sodden turf squelched underfoot.

"Watch where you put your dogs," Bob was saying. "It's not far. This way. Follow me."

His voice might have been that of a professional guide. We walked between two rows of stalls. The lights were going out, one by one. The whole place was closing for the night.

"Tough on them," Leslie was saying.

"Up this road now," Bob said. "It's not far."

He was walking in front, quickly. Leslie and the kid followed. I tailed along. The air after the rain was pleasant, like air blown in off the sea at night, and the rustling hedges on either side of the road dripped softly.

"Is there a pub near the picture house?" Leslie said.

I didn't catch Bob's answer. At the end of the road lights were showing, a high light standard and windows like square eyes.

"Not far now," Bob said, moving one dark finger across his putty-coloured throat. It was like the underside of a tortoise. His grey suede shoes were black with rain.

I was walking back along the main street, which was nearly deserted. The canal bank would be deserted too. Gravel and rain. The deck of the barge would be slippery. I felt free for the first time since early morning. For me there had been a nightmare aspect about the fair, a private melodrama; I had been contained without being caught up in something which had nothing to do with me, and, being so involved, was cut off from myself, my own direction. And now suddenly, as soon as I left the others, I was conscious of being coerced no longer, and the world came to exist for me again, not as a foreign element to be looked at, but as a climate in which

79

I could become immersed, whose parts were merely an extension of myself, or, the same thing, were continuous with me and I with them.

It had got colder. I buttoned up my jacket as I walked. I remembered the crinkling blonde hair of the woman who had stood opposite me inside the stall and then the birdlike jerk of the tramp. It was then that it occurred to me it was the dead woman he reminded me of. Something missing. And what remained implied what was missing.

The rain was still off. I passed the public urinal. I felt somehow a hostility in the glances of the few loungers who hung about it. It struck me as strange how they chose to stand there, alone or in small groups, smoking, idling away the time. One of them laughed. He had made some comment or other which I didn't catch. A policeman passed me on a bicycle. Funny – I *always* notice policemen. The tyres swished on the wet road, sending up sprinkles of dirty water, and his cloak blew out like a tent behind him. I supposed he was going home.

Then I was returning down the road between the hedges. Hawthorn, I think. I could hear them dripping on the grass and bracken at either side of me. A cat rose from the ditch, darted across the road, and went through the hedge at the other side. Someone was walking in front of me, going in the same direction. I knew that because his footsteps didn't get any louder. I wondered who it was. I slowed down until he had passed out of earshot. Not far then. I passed the fairground. Of course. That was where he was going. A few lights were still burning. I heard a woman's laugh. It was not unlike Ella's, flung and uncontrolled, the laughter of the slums. Farther on, I heard two men talking quietly behind the hedge. By the time I reached the canal everything was silent except for the ambiguous presence of the canal itself. There is a noise that is peculiar to inland water at night, a kind of radiation that is not exactly sound and not exactly smell; it is closer to touch; its being touches one at the pores. There was no one on the footpaths. I walked carefully along the path and boarded the barge.

It was dark in the cabin and deadly quiet except for the tick of the clock over their bunk. She had gone to bed.

I moved with my hands in front of me like a blind man. I found a chair and sat down on it. As my eyes became accustomed to the dark I became aware of Ella's breathing. She was in the big bunk and somehow I was convinced she was not asleep. She must have known it was I. She must have heard me come down through the companionway.

"Ella!" My voice wasn't loud.

She didn't answer. Dimly the clock face reflected what seemed to be an eternity behind the glass, as though there were a tunnel there leading into an obscure distance. I saw Ella's shape under the blanket, the edge of the table, the paraffin lamp, dark masses of varying densities at my elbows and at my feet and at the other side of the cabin. A shaft of lesser darkness came down through the companionway.

"Ella!" Louder this time.

I put out my hand and touched her shoulder. It was only then that I realized she was crying, not loudly, but softly into the pillow. I could not see why. My fingers, conscious of their own awkwardness now, were still on her shoulder.

At that moment she moved her arm.

"Go away, Joe! I don't want to see you!"

"You're mad," I said uncertainly. I was mystified.

"Go away, Joe!"

"For God's sake!"

As I said it I stepped backwards and my arm caught the long globe of the oil lamp which tilted and fell over. The glass splintered as it crashed on to the deck.

"Now look what you've done!" She sat up.

"I can't see a bloody thing," I said. "Wait till I strike a match."

Ella swung herself off the bunk.

"Give them to me," she said sharply, "and stand back out of the way until I clear it up."

I felt her snatch the matchbox from my hand and a fraction of a second later a match splurted into flame between her fingers. In the sudden, brief eruption of the match I could see her clearly, her shadow on the woodwork, and the clock with its brass ring. At that moment it struck nine, its small, brassy chime magnified by the artificiality of the situation. The match went out and she lit another. She was bending, trying to see where the lamp had fallen. The cabin smelled overpoweringly of paraffin.

"It's leaking," she said.

"Have you not got a candle?"

"Jim used the last one. I meant to get some."

She didn't appear to be aware I was watching her. She was wearing a very loose white slip which hung on loose strings from her shoulders so that I could see the rise of her breasts and their corkish nipples clearly in the match light. The slip clung tightly about her relaxed belly and stopped just short of her knees like a badly-fitting curtain. Her thick, fleshy legs were planted firmly on broad feet on the wooden planks of the deck and her heavy upper arm slewed from side to side as she cupped her hands round the match to direct its beam downwards. I noticed that she had a mole on her side, almost under the armpit where the hairs grew thickly and twisted into wisps. She smelled warm, of sleep-sweat, of the bed.

"Watch your feet," I said gently. "You'll get them cut."

She located the lamp.

"Can you see where the brush is?" she said, turning towards me.

I was barring her way.

"Joe…"

"They won't be back for a couple of hours at least," I said. "I left them in a cinema."

She was going to protest but when I moved against her she drew in her breath instead. I held her firmly against me, my thumbs under her armpits, massaging the damp hairs, my fingers like claws at the soft flesh of her shoulders. She didn't resist. My hands dropped to her haunches, pulling her to me, so that her thick abdomen came hard against my own clothed body. She buried her head at my shoulder.

Afterwards, as we lay in each other's arms beneath the rough blanket (she wouldn't hear of our going between the sheets), the sides of her abdomen and her flanks were covered in a thin lather of sweat. We breathed in and out together, deeply, so that our bodies met together and fell away again, leaving a slight prickle on the skin.

Outside, it began to rain. We could hear its hushed fall on the water, the gravel, the wood. It was there with our breathing, a curtain of sound, something beyond us to which we both listened as, with our eyes open, and with our own thoughts, we looked at one another in the dark.

Part Two

1

G O BACK TO THE BEGINNING.
  It's an odd thing, or rather it *was* an odd thing. Thank God it's not likely to happen again.

I wanted to talk about Ella, about how she suddenly came to me, like a brainwave, on the very day we dragged the dead woman from the river. For that reason, and not to complicate the issue, I said nothing about Cathie. At least I didn't show where she fitted into the picture. She was there all the time of course, but you didn't know it. She was the corpse.

I nearly said *my* corpse. But a corpse, strictly speaking, doesn't belong to anyone, and though I could have laid some claim to her body while it lived, I like to think I have no claim, not even a murderer's, on her corpse.

I killed Cathie. There's no point in denying it since no one would believe me. The police, with their usual sensationalism, began at once to investigate the possibility of foul play. That was according to the newspapers. What it meant in fact was that they were already looking for a murderer. Well, they found one, but we'll come to that later. What convinced them, I suppose, was the fact that she was wearing no clothes. That, they no doubt felt, indicated the presence of a man. At least one man. I'm with them there, of course. It's the kind of conclusion I might jump to myself. You too, perhaps. But the assumption that because a man has sexual intercourse with a woman in somewhat unseemly circumstances, because later the woman's body is found floating in one of our navigable rivers – the assumption that the man did her in afterwards seems to me to be entirely without justification.

The newspapers, conscious of their status as guardians of public morals, encouraged the idea. The general public swallowed it greedily. Leslie believed. Bob believed. Ella believed. So I went on keeping my mouth shut.

Go back to the beginning, the one I chose, though I might have gone back a year or even ten to find the beginnings of it all, to that morning we dragged her from the river. It was an odd thing that I, who saw Cathie topple into the river, should have been the one to find her body the following morning at one mile's distance from where she fell in. I felt at the time that it was ludicrous, so incredible that if Leslie had not happened to come up on deck at the time I should most certainly have refused to accept such an improbable event and tried to thrust her away again with the boat-hook.

Unfortunately, Leslie slouched up at the wrong moment and it occurred to him on seeing the body in the water that it was our duty to fish it out. At least that's what he said.

The face of the man in the cloth cap came into the news between an air crash, forty-seven dead, and a financial conference to be held in Paris. The dotted image was set obscurely in the page, a glint of white in a host of darker dots, as though the face were trying to sink into the background and merge with it. The caption underneath read:

CLYDE MURDER
Man charged
Daniel Goon, plumber, of 42 Black Street, Glasgow, was today remanded in custody at the Central Police Court. He is charged with the murder of Catherine Dimly, 27, sometime actress, of 2, Noble Grove, Glasgow. Goon is the father of four children. Miss Dimly's body was discovered two weeks ago by two bargemen who recovered it from the River Clyde.

I found it difficult to conceive what evidence they could have against Goon. Goon had nothing to do with it. And I was quite convinced that I had destroyed all possible evidence.

When Cathie tripped and fell backwards into the river the scream choked in her throat before it was uttered and then the lights on the opposite shore were winking and everything seemed deadly quiet. The splash was contained inside my head for a few moments, like a cry in a wood, before I lay down flat on the quay in a movement of panic and stared down at the quick black water. It sidled swiftly past the quay stones and a few yards away, quietly at the surface, a few bubbles broke, like suds from a laundry, farther and farther away until there was nothing to be seen.

I knew at once that she was dead, gone, beyond all help, at once and at the same time as the knowledge of the paralysis of my limbs came to me. I remained where I was without moving for a long time, my eyes after the hour we had spent together well-accustomed to the dark, and first there was a matchbox and then a bottle and then a spar of wood, and each object made a different noise as it scraped past the stones and disappeared in the flow of the current. I thought of stars hurtling away from one another in the black universe beyond the speed of light.

And then I was thinking that Cathie was down there somewhere.

It was too dark and it was too late to do anything. Scream now? I looked for a trace of her for a long time but, except for the debris that was floating past, the water was evenly dark, and after a while it struck me that what I was trying to do was like trying to pin the tail on the donkey behind the sheet. She might have been anywhere, at any level. Christ!

I remember a feeling of disbelief. How quickly it had happened, with nothing to lead up to it. Nothing. To me it was as unreasonable as an earthquake on an English lawn. Later, that was what was to strike me as so fraudulent about the prosecutor's point-by-point reconstruction. At the moment she fell there was no great passion in either of us. There wasn't even a scream, no frantic hand in the water, and, on my side, I was surprised how quickly I became calm. Did I believe she had swum a distance under water and reached the bank farther down? I knew she hadn't. I knew she couldn't swim. She had always been afraid of the water. I used to tease her about it sometimes when we went out in a rowing boat. A summer's day perhaps, not far from shore somewhere off the west coast, and we would be lying naked on the bottom boards under the seats. She was more passionate that way than any other, because she knew she couldn't swim, because our erotic struggle in the drifting boat represented for her a life and death matter. It was not only her body which prostrated itself in the flimsy shell of the dinghy. It was her life she gambled with, uttering little screams of delirious pleasure when a chance wave decapitated itself on the gunwale and splashed like quicksilver about her buttocks. She said she felt the power of the sea through the wood of the boat in her flesh as well as in her ears and that she never felt she was giving herself so utterly as when, her muscles taut on the rutted bottom-boards, the bows lifted and a spray of water landed like chill grapeshot against her thighs.

Gradually I became used to the idea that she was drowned, beyond help, and somehow the quiet lap of water against the stones was reassuring to me – more than that, it had a positive fascination for me. Undoubtedly it was because of the kind of compact which had always existed between our mating and the water. She attained to an ecstasy through terror of it, and on more than one occasion she said, even if thereby she was simply giving in to her penchant for melodrama, she felt that was how she would die, overtaken in sex by water. She was not entirely mistaken.

If a policeman had come along at that moment I should probably have made no move to escape. It was only later, after a few minutes, that I realized my own position was dangerous, that there was only

PART TWO · CHAPTER 1

my word for it that it was an accident. Or was it an accident? I suppose it was. It had never occurred to me to kill her. I was merely walking away. She tried to hold me back. I extricated myself. She lost her balance. She tripped over a cobblestone and then she was in the water. Splash. It all happened so quickly.

Perhaps some people would say I was to blame because my reactions were so slow. I must have willed her death. I don't think so. Although certainly the feeling uppermost in my mind when she toppled backwards was that of annoyance. I *was* annoyed with her. And then a kind of panic-tinged curiosity. She was gone suddenly, and as my anger evaporated I became breathlessly curious, and then a wave of fear that was almost nausea came over me, and I was lying down staring at the water where she had disappeared. If only she had broken the surface, even for an instant, I might have moved. But somehow or other from the very beginning I felt it was hopeless, done rather, and at that moment I cannot honestly say I cared very much, though I did afterwards when I realized she was dead. Dead. Dead. Dead. My mother and now Cathie. As surprising as forked lightning. And then the gradual expansion as, caught up in my imagination, the dull red fact expanded like a painful sunrise over the whole horizon.

Say I was involved in a state of quiet shock, at the edge of apprehension, soothed by the water as it swirled indolently past the slime-covered quay stones. The seconds marked themselves out with the disappearance of the bubbles, and with the appearance of the matchbox, the bottle, the spar, a hunk of rotting cork, and three minutes at least must have passed before I felt my sense of personal danger. That came suddenly as the accident itself, as though a trapdoor all at once opened into a deeper consciousness of the situation, and my eyes left the surface of the water and moved across the flickering breadth of the river to the other side where the lights still winked in a kind of cynical confederacy. I felt very alone then, an alien, an exile, society already crystallizing against me, and only my own desperate word for what had happened.

I was now in a kneeling position on the cobblestones and I could feel their cold hardness at my kneecaps. I stood up and as I did so my eyes caught sight of the bundle of clothes she had so willingly taken off for me. They were lying close to the wheel of the railway truck under which we had made love. The siding was right on the quay. We had both of us thought it was a good place.

It was then it occurred to me that things would have looked better for me if she had had her clothes on when she fell in. The furtive sexuality of the situation would tend to make it appear criminal. I had the absurd idea of finding the body and dressing it in the clothes. That struck me as funny a moment later. I picked up the clothes and looked at them. They were evidence. Naturally, I had to get rid of them.

It did not occur to me to go to the police but I saw no reason why they should accept my version of the incident. I always say the wrong things at interviews. I dislike the way most other people expect me to share their attitudes. I could imagine their questioning me about Cathie, the loaded questions they would thrust at me. I dismissed the thought of going to the police almost as soon as it occurred to me.

There was no hurry. There was no sign of anyone about. I decided to smoke a cigarette and think the whole thing over carefully.

The cigarette made me feel better. I was not going to do anything much. The clothes were there, still slightly warm under my hand. Or was that an illusion? I decided to think the whole thing out in detail before deciding on my course of action. Part of me began almost to enjoy the situation. It had been forced upon me without logic, like Mexico on Maximilian; it was up to me to accept my predicament and to free myself of the implications. Good. It was like a game of chess. I ground the stub of my cigarette on the stone. My hand had hardly left it when my fingers felt for it again almost reflectively. That too, I supposed was evidence. I smiled then. It was a good thing I had smoked a cigarette. Somewhere under the truck were two other cigarette butts and one would have lipstick on it. I repressed the urge to look for them at once. Take it easy. Plenty of time. Oh, Cathie! The main thing was not to commit myself to any unanalysed act however slight it might seem and to destroy scientifically the absurd complex in which I had become involved.

I had got myself involved, absurdly and without forethought. For I had met Cathie in the street, quite by accident, after a period of two months during which I had neither seen her nor written to her (in fact I had left her, or she had left me, *quien sabe?*) and our decision to make love had been sudden, impulsive, as decision sometimes is, taken while seated in an alcove in a small café, where we had gone for coffee. I simply took her hand. And it was as though we had never separated. The gesture brought back a hundred memories, of nights during which we had lain in one another's arms, of thighs insistently interlocked, of happy laughter.

We had known each other for a long time. We did not need to speak about it. A glance was enough, a slight flush of excitement on her cheeks, a responsive pressure of the hand. She would if I suggested it. We left the café and walked straight towards the river. She had a room mate now.

The proprietor of the café was an old Italian who sat on a high stool behind the counter. He had glanced at us without interest, as later, while we were drinking coffee, he had looked at the wall with the faded harlequins which happened to be opposite him. He said good night as we left, indolently, or mechanically. He might have recognized me again but there was little likelihood of his being called upon to do so. As far as he was concerned, I judged, there was nothing to be afraid of. And unless we had been seen by someone who knew us both he appeared to be the only possible witness. We had met two streets away from the café, walked there together, and then, when we came out again, we had gone quickly along the dark streets which led to the river. Possibly we were seen. But as I smoked my second cigarette I became certain that we weren't. It was dark when we met. We crossed only one main street in a city of more than a million inhabitants. A tree hidden in the forest…

No connection for over two months. For the world, for our mutual acquaintances, we were separated. She had had no opportunity to speak to anyone of our meeting. The element of chance had worked for as well as against me. There was no point in going to the police. It wouldn't do Cathie any good. She had no relatives, only me, as I already knew. I began to pity her then. It had been so sudden, so fraudulent, and she had been laughing a few minutes before. Christ! But going to the police was out. It might involve me, fatally.

What about the clothes? ("Let me take them off," she had said. I was surprised at first but then I realized what it was she wanted. It would give her pleasure to feel the wood of the sleeper and the gravel under her. I remember the whiteness of her hips against the dark wood. Looking up above my shoulder she must have seen the oily underside of the truck. How to explain all that to the police? To a jury of twelve good men and true?)

I was sorry now that she taken her clothes off. If she had been fully dressed she would not have been in such a hurry to stop me as I walked away. The whole thing might never have happened. And now the clothes were a problem.

Not much of a problem though. If there was nothing to connect me with her, then her clothes were irrelevant. The police might as well have them. (This proved to be a mistake.) They would miss them anyway. The coroner's verdict would be "murder by person or persons unknown". Some impulse made me throw the clothes into one of the trucks. Afterwards I wondered why I had done it. And I even thought of climbing in to retrieve them. But I thought: "You are becoming hysterical." Perhaps I derived a sense of having gambled from this act in spite of the fact that the clothes were irrelevant anyway. I didn't bother to go after them. But there was the handbag. I had touched that, so there would be fingerprints on it. Elementary, my dear. I rubbed the smooth surface briskly with my handkerchief before finding a large stone, weighting the handbag with it, and throwing far out into the water. That took care of that, doubly. And then I was suddenly annoyed with myself. There was a Ronson cigarette-lighter in the handbag and I had touched that too. Two for one against. But the bag would probably never be found – "till a' the seas gang dry…"

My sense of tidiness made me search for the cigarette stubs. It was fortunate I did so. I found her packet of Player's and the cigarette-lighter too. I was pleased about that. The cigarette-lighter had been my only oversight, and lying there under the truck for anyone to see and pick up it might have been decisive – certainly, because of the monogram, if the body was identified. I wiped it carefully with my handkerchief and hurled it as far as I could. I listened for the plop, thinking of St Mungo and the fish. Mouth open, fish. I saw no point in wasting the cigarettes. I transferred what remained (seven) to my own box and dropped the empty packet into the river. I found the two stubs and did the same with them. After that there was nothing else to be done. Perhaps an hour had passed since Cathie had disappeared in the water. If not at the beginning, it was certainly too late now. In my hesitation did I commit murder?

I stepped close to the edge for the last time and looked down at the water. Still no sign of her. The water was smooth and black with lights like fish scales glimmering where a street- or bridge-lamp was reflected, smooth as though smoothed by a plasterer's trowel, and inscrutable. Behind me, the line of railway trucks stood silent and abandoned, blockish like cows in the dark, with their wheels at rest and their couplings like tails dangling loose, screening me with their immobility from the movement of the city. They seemed bigger than they were, prehistoric cows, and their immobility communicated itself to me. I felt vaguely that the whole incident had taken place out of time, that there had been a break in continuity, that what happened was not part of my history. It was pervaded with the unreality of fiction, dream. I would wake up soon. I had merely to walk away to free myself from an obsession.

Nevertheless I found myself walking carefully to the shadow of the line of trucks, articulating, without voice: "Thou sure and firm-set earth, hear not my step… for fear the very stones…" I did not wish to be seen coming away from the spot. As I crossed the rails behind the last truck it came to me that anyway I had never told Cathie my real name. She knew me as Joe Taylor. I always gave my correct Christian name because it's difficult to remember and react normally to an incorrect one. Perhaps in her room there would be a few photographs, not many, because I never liked having my photograph taken, but one or two, and that worried me. Still, it wasn't likely they would look very hard for Joe Taylor. Those who knew us knew we had separated over two months before, by mutual agreement, not in anger. True? False? Anyway, I had not seen any of them since.

I reached the street without being seen. I passed only one man in the dark streets which led to the centre of the city, and then, by another route altogether, I made my way back to the river and the barge. Ella – as yet Leslie's wife only – was awake when I got back.

"That you, Joe?" she called from the bunk.

In the darkness I heard Leslie's snore.

"Yes," I said.

"Fine time to be coming back here! What d'you think this is? A doss house?"

I didn't reply.

When I got into my bunk I felt sad, and a little frightened. Christ! Why? That it couldn't have happened, and certainly without it ever occurring to me to frame the possibility, that it couldn't be that I would ever see Cathie again.

2

THE FACTS WERE NOT MADE PUBLIC at that time. I could get no information from the newspapers beyond the fact that the plumber had been charged with murder. I assumed that investigations were still being made and the lack of information in the press made me uneasy.

When I considered the whole thing calmly I saw no reason why I should even be questioned, far less suspected, but as the days passed and no new reference was made to the crime in the newspapers and the silence struck me as ominous, and the fact that I could make no move myself to find out what was happening without running the risk of bringing attention on myself made things worse.

I wanted to act. I had an illogical fear that I had left something undone and that by so doing I had committed myself unknowingly, but to what circumstances or line of action I had no idea. There was nothing to do but wait. The silence couldn't last indefinitely. Sooner or later they would have to bring the plumber to trial. For the present there was no moment at which I could say with certainty that I was in more (or less) danger than I had been the moment before, and this inability to localize in time, place, or person, a concrete threat, made me morose and uncommunicative. Sometimes in the street I had the impression I was being followed, and I would turn off, double back on my tracks, come to an abrupt halt, board a moving bus. But in calm moments I dismissed this idea as unrealistic. Once they connected me with the affair they would take me in for questioning. There would be no beating about the bush.

I found it impossible to think of the plight of Goon out of relation to myself. Poor bastard, there was no point in my exaggerating my sympathy for him. I didn't even know him. As a representative of the industrious working classes he was in a sense my enemy. I dislike people who make a virtue of work. And in a way he was a part, if an uncritical one, of the society which might condemn him in a sense in which I was not. I knew he was innocent certainly. But so was I. I couldn't establish his innocence without convicting myself. The position might have been reversed. In an absurd way we were rivals; if one of us were condemned the other would go free. His arrest too was no more absurd than the position which would be thrust upon me by an unintelligent society perennially bent on its moral purification: "What! She didn't have her knickers on!" When I thought of Goon I thought of him as part of a vast octopus organism which, spotlighting an individual cell, called that cell bad. Poor Goon was bad. The newspapers implied it. If he was convicted the judge would pronounce it. And the octopus would strangle him. Goon would know that he was not bad, but no doubt he would be convinced that someone else was bad, I, for example, though for him I was nameless. I still pitied him in spite of the fact that he thought I was bad. That didn't make him bad, nor even the octopus; they were simply unintelligent. Both Goon and I were victims of that, and only one of us could escape. Of course we might both have escaped. The police might have accepted my account of the incident. But there was a strong possibility that they wouldn't. I couldn't take the chance. My responsibility in the matter was simply a convenient social fiction, one which had shamed God knows how many men into assisting at their own murder.

It was not my sympathy for the plumber which took me to Black Street. I was drawn there in the vague hope of finding out something which would make my own position clearer. Somewhere, perhaps at that very moment, a clerk in a police station would be fingering a sheaf of documents. Later, he would walk along a corridor in some building or other and put the file on someone's desk. The anonymity of the men who at that very moment might be working against me not because they had a personal grudge against me but because they were part of an impersonal machine whose function it was to maintain order, to explain the presence of an ambiguous thing like a corpse, to see that, if foul play was deduced, someone atoned for it that the moral structure of the system might be preserved – that was horrifying. These men, whoever they were, would sleep with their wives, take their children for a picnic on Sundays, mention casually to a friend that investigations were proceeding satisfactorily, much in the same way as they might talk about a crossword puzzle. There was something nightmarish about it – my nightmare, for the machine might include me in its intricate pattern-making at any moment.

I walked to the end of the street and back again. It was a short street of tenements in a poor quarter of the town, bleak and grey, and looked like any one of the streets surrounding it. There was nothing to see: few men, shambling women wrapped in shawls. I looked up as the shrill cry of a woman issued from one of the windows. She was leaning over the sill, her flat, red, suspicious face craning out from the window above her flaccid breasts like some grotesque figurehead. She clutched a towel to her breast in a thin red hand. Her mouth hung open as though to receive the reply of the woman to whom she had called, a short, stout woman, hatless, with bare pink legs and broken shoes, clutching a baby in a grey shawl about her. I felt depressed. I turned away. A coal cart moved slowly towards me at the other side, but there was nothing special about the Clydesdale horse which hauled it nor about the man who walked beside it, who, as it had now begun to rain, wore an empty coal bag like a monk's cowl at his head and shoulders. He walked in front of the horse and slightly to one side of it, shuffling his big boots along the gutter.

Above, a ribbon of white sky, just beginning to be overclouded, from which rain fell in slender, broken javelins. I felt the first drops break on the shoulder of my blue serge jacket. My hair didn't get wet, for that day I was wearing one of Leslie's cloth caps as a badge of my insignificance. There was no sign of a policeman. The street that had housed and would if necessary sacrifice a murderer to society at large bore no singular mark of its distinction. No black or yellow cross was painted at the close numbered 42. No curious group gathered nearby to talk of omens. I stood out of the rain in a close near the corner a dozen yards away for about ten minutes, smoked a cigarette, trying to absorb something, I don't know what, and felt foolish and vaguely false. There was nothing to be done. I had no plan in mind. It had occurred to me to visit a neighbourhood bar on the off chance that I might overhear something, anything. But when I got there I didn't feel like it. Some kids were coming home from school, kicking an empty can along the street, and I wondered if any of them were his kids. That made me wonder what it would mean to them now to have Goon as a father. If a policeman had been shot, or even a man knifed in the street, the kids might have turned the notoriety to some account. But a sex crime was something shameful like a bad smell. It was tough on the kids. It must have occurred to me vaguely that I might catch a glimpse of the wife: fat, thin, scrawny, red, bow-legged? What was she thinking? Would she stand by him? There must have been some connection between Goon and Cathie, or they wouldn't have arrested him. I wondered what it was. It seemed to me he must have been her lover. It puzzled me. A plumber, Goon. Married with four children. And Cathie, whose father had been a minor civil servant with the Post Office or something, an eager representative of possibly the most class-conscious of all British classes, whose influence she had never quite thrown off. I was very curious about this. It would come out if and when there was a trial, how they had met, some of the particulars of their relationship. Cathie hadn't mentioned him to me. It might have been Goon's child. It gave me a strange feeling to know that I would never know whose child died with her in the river. I forgot to remind you, Cathie was pregnant.

I walked away at last out of that part of the town. The rain had stopped abruptly. It was still early in the evening and I didn't feel like going back to the barge. Ella would be there, alone probably, or with the kid. Leslie might still be knocking about. More likely he was in one of the dockside pubs, playing darts, or if no one would play with him, dominoes. I didn't want to see Ella at that moment.

I wondered how much of a coincidence it was that I first made love with Ella on the day Cathie's body came floating back to me like a little hunk of synthetic guilt. I wondered how much I was moved by an instinctive need of a woman at the precise moment, on that precise day, because I was suddenly an outlaw beyond any intellectual and voluntary commission, not for now but *from now on*. If I went to the police with my story of what happened, and if I were very lucky, I might get off with manslaughter, though the temper of the good people, citizens of the Presbyterian city of Glasgow, their moral appetites already whetted, made me have a second thought about that. My sudden need of Ella the day after Cathie died and after many months of living close to her in a state of detached unaffection, and the fact that the power of seduction came with the need, that I discovered in every successive response a sense of control in myself and of her permissiveness – this complex knowledge gave me a sense of vast gravitational forces which went beyond any "I" I was conscious of, of a complexly woven matrix within which my own conscious decisions were mere threads.

I didn't want to see Ella because she was becoming demanding and less and less cautious. She wanted me to make love to her at every odd moment, and when I protested it was too risky she laughed at me. I think she almost wanted Leslie to find out about us.

"Who's scared now?" she said.

There was nothing I could say.

One time the four of us went for a picnic and Leslie and the kid went off to get water to make the tea. They were hardly out of sight when she pulled me over on top of her. I made love to her quickly, almost passionately, and I had just broken loose when Leslie and the kid came into sight with the water. That kind of thing happened often and I began to realize it was only a question of time before Leslie found out. Ella knew that too. It increased her pleasure. Her attitude was infectious and I entered into the spirit of the affair almost because in doing so I was able to forget the other more serious threat which the silence of the newspapers seemed to signify.

Ella's body continued to excite me. When she made love now she gave herself to me completely, almost hysterically.

So I returned that night only a few hours after I had left Black Street and she was waiting for me as I knew she would be. I felt in some undefined way resigned. The days passed and through her I lived out a life that was separate and intact, with its own force and its own risk and its own centre. Gradually, until the day when it fell to pieces, I began to forget that I had been with Cathie when she fell backwards into the river and that there was any connection between the woman who had been my mistress and the drowned woman towards whom I reached with the boat hook. I didn't think of Goon. He bored me. And then, one day, Leslie discovered us.

Ella had ceased to move. Her eyes were closed and she was breathing heavily. Inside me, a recession was taking place, the sensation of closeness was evaporating. The image sharpened. She was merely a woman with whom I had just made love. Her body was soft, putty-like, unexhilarating, out of tune.

The weight of her thigh on my knee was uncomfortable. I had a slight headache. The clock with the brass ring ticked loudly, stabilizing the atmosphere in the cabin and drawing all objects back to their accustomed banality. The quilt was merely a quilt which had been washed too often. The varnished planks did not fit tightly together and the varnish looked unsmooth and brittle. For the last few minutes I had been conscious of the buzz of a fly and now it alighted on Ella's shoulder and walked towards the nipple of her right breast. She appeared to be unaware of it. Her head leant over to the side and the hairs on her temple were stringy with perspiration. There was a faint smile on her lips as though she were thinking of something which amused her. Her satisfaction seemed inane. The fact that she had withdrawn and remained confident with her eyes shut annoyed me. Her attitude was ridiculous, insulting. She appeared ridiculous to me with her smirk of withdrawal, her white flesh patched red where it had been crushed under my weight and with the fly at her nipple, hesitating, flexing its minute feelers, like a minute chef preparing to carve up a turkey.

"When will Leslie be back?" I said.

She opened her eyes and looked at me. At that moment the fly rose into the air and disappeared somewhere against the dark brown varnish of the planks. She was smiling.

"Not for a while yet."

She put out her arm and drew me down to her again. I resisted slightly but she was determined. Her mouth was soft and too wet. I closed my teeth against her tongue. But without exerting myself I couldn't get free and so I closed my eyes and allowed her to go on kissing my neck and my cheeks. After a while my resentment seemed to move outside me and to stand off at a distance, until, when her fingers moved at me again, it sank away like the light of a buoy below the horizon and I was no longer conscious of it. I felt no urgency at first, but gradually my submission ceased to be passive only, and I found myself making love to her again.

Afterwards we were both tired and we fell asleep.

Leslie must have come down to the cabin and when he saw us he must have gone on deck again. When we awoke it was nearly dark and we could hear him walking back and forth on the deck above us. We listened for a while without moving. Neither of us had any idea how long he had been there, but he was obviously waiting for us to wake up, letting us know by his walking there that he knew and at the same time giving us an opportunity to prepare ourselves before we faced him. We spoke in whispers.

"Do you think he knows?"

"Of course he does!" I said. I lit a cigarette.

"What'll we do?"

I smiled in the dark.

"I suppose that depends on him."

Ella did not answer for a moment and then she said: "Why should it depend on him? Who the hell does he think he is anyway? Clumping around up there like the Day of Judgement!"

"It's only his way of letting us know he's there."

"He's done it," she said drily.

She was waiting for me to say or do something and she moved slightly so that no part of our bodies was touching under the rough blanket, which seemed rougher and more prickly now than it had before; but I saw only the end of my cigarette glowing in the dark and somehow that seemed to fill my mind, that and the shadows beyond it, excluding any immediate adjustment to the situation. Anyway, I knew without discussing it with her that if Leslie had been going to do anything rash he would have done it by now and that he was probably as nervous as we were about what was going to happen when we met again.

"Are you just going to lie there?"

"There's no hurry," I said, "I'll finish my cigarette."

"What is there to say?"

"The whole thing's pretty obvious, isn't it?"

She moved again, but she did not speak. I thought for a moment that she was going to climb out over me, but she must have changed her mind for some reason or other. In moving she had pulled the blanket off my right side, which was at the edge of the bed. She wanted me to move. Reluctantly, I lowered myself on the deck, struck a match and lit the oil lamp, and then, without looking at her, I began to dress.

Leslie must have become conscious of the light in the cabin because a few moments later he stopped walking backwards and forwards on deck, and for a moment I almost expected him to come down through the companionway and I pulled on my trousers quickly so as to be in a better position to face up to him, but he did not come, didn't even call down to us, and Ella's voice said then: "He's waiting for you to go up."

I did not answer her. I wasn't in the mood to discuss it, to talk at all. Now that it had happened, the thought of the other danger came back to me. It was as though, unconsciously, I had all the time associated the two threats, as though, since they were almost coeval, they had lain on me together, apocalyptically implying one another, point for point, and now that one threat had been realized a corresponding development in the other was threatening – at that very moment perhaps, the official in charge of investigations into Cathie's death would be noticing for the first time a connection between the deceased and one of the bargemen who had discovered the body; or perhaps it was merely that the world of Ella and Leslie (for both of whom the incident was now closed) in which to the exclusion of the other I had been able to involve myself, like an invalid in the routine of the sickroom, was no longer, since Leslie had found out about us, separate and self-contained. I remember that my mouth was dry then. I had been thirsty before I fell asleep, and I lifted the milk which had been on the table since early afternoon and drank a deep draught from the bottle.

Ella watched me but said nothing. She was withdrawn in a different way now, and it was I who was being looked at. That made me uncomfortable. I had no idea what she was thinking as she lay there on her side, supported by her elbow, watching me dress, with her eyes in shadow back somewhere behind and above her protruding lips. Her neck and the top part of her body, which was relaxed heavily on the under-sheet were an ochrous colour in the lamplight which, radiating through the tall, no longer clear globe from one hard bright tongue of flame, lighted my tagless shoelace under my fingertips. I remained bent longer than necessary and the hair on my naked arms looked grey and the flesh dirty where the veins rose near the surface like a geographical complex of contours. It occurred to me that I hadn't had a bath for over a week.

When I had tied my shoelaces I slipped my shirt over my head and while I was buttoning it I looked at Ella.

"Are you getting up too?"

"Maybe," she said. "I'll wait and see what happens. Look. Your cigarette. It's burning the table."

A long bow of ash fell on the floor as I lifted it to stub it smouldering on the ashtray. I lifted my jacket from the back of the chair and put it on.

"I'll see what he says, then," I said, more because I felt I had to say something before going on deck than because she needed to be told that. I think she laughed then as I turned and climbed up through the companionway.

When I returned to the cabin about fifteen minutes later a tremorous black thread of oil smoke was suspended between the scored globe and a spot on the bulkhead where the fine particles of soot densened and wavered in a flat, spider-like cloud, while the globe itself, a chancre of red and yellow and black in suppuration, gave less and less light on to the table and the bed where Ella, who had not moved since I left her, lay half-naked on her elbow with the blanket fallen away to the level of her navel. The cabin was already in semi-darkness but it did not seem to concern her. She had made no effort to reach out and turn the lamp down or to trim the wick. Instead she had watched as the arc of light moved away from her centripetally towards the smoking orange eye of flame, which flickered as I climbed down through the companionway as though it were trying to draw all the light in the cabin back into itself. I turned it down and for a moment the room was in almost total darkness.

"You'll have to trim the wick," Ella's voice said to me from the bunk, and, as I burned my fingertips when I tried to remove the hot globe, she said: "There's a dishcloth behind you. Use that."

She did not speak again until I had pinched away the burnt part of the wick between my thumb and forefinger, relit the lamp and replaced the globe. The lamp was now burning rather dully because the globe was dirty.

"You might have turned it down," I said.

"It'll clean," she said shortly.

And I supposed it would clean. That was part of Ella, to be cleaning things, dishes or shoes or the table, scouring pots and pans, polishing brasses, which she did with a special cloth, blowing her hot breath on to the metal and then making it squeak under the friction of the cloth, her big forearm moving backwards and forwards like a piston whose energy you could almost see being drained from the tensed stock of her body and from the rigid stance of her powerful haunches on which the apron string, idle and discoloured, always lay.

Then I lit a cigarette and, crossing my legs, sat down at a distance from her. She appeared to be content to wait for me to tell her what had happened. Knowing what had happened and the uselessness of any effort on our part to alter it, I was not in a hurry to speak. I had half-finished my cigarette before she decided that she had waited long enough.

"Where is he?"

"He's gone," I said.

"Where for Heaven's sake?"

"God knows," I said. "I suppose he'll stop at a men's club tonight and go to his mother's in Glasgow in the morning."

"Did he say he was leaving me?"

"He said he would write you a letter."

"Cripes!"

She clambered bigly and whitely from the bunk, the soles of her feet making a flat stabbing sound on the boards as she landed on the deck. She brushed past me, leaving her odour as she crossed the cabin to the stove, and to see her close, suddenly like that, naked flesh in flat surface not six inches from my eye which received the impression in a neutral, emotionless way, was in a new way terrifying, because the flesh which I thought I knew, had touched and held under the pressure of my fingertips, was presented anonymously as an amorphous mass of grey-white, yellowing at its edges, and pitted like pumice-stone, a mass which lost its identity and its momentary passage in front of my eye, and, a fraction of a second later, was gone and replaced by an odour in my nostrils which grew familiar, of woman, as I moved my head to watch Ella arrive at the stove, strike a match, and place the kettle on the lighted gas ring. The new sound, the thrust of the ignited gas, seemed to restore equilibrium to the cabin, to make of Ella again a woman with a tendency to fatness who no longer considered it necessary to cover herself in front of me.

"Cripes!" she said again. "So he's going to write me a letter!"

"That's what he said."

"Do you want a cup of tea?" She was smiling now.

"I could do with one."

"Me too," she said, and then: "It looks as though we've settled for one another, Joe!"

I didn't know what else I could do other than to laugh pleasantly. I brayed like an ass.

She reached for the tea caddy.

3

DURING THE DAYS THAT FOLLOWED, we remained tied up at Leith. Leslie sent a boy to fetch his things and Ella picked up her kid, who had been staying for a few days with her step-sister, Gwendoline, whose husband was a lorry-driver for a firm of fruit and vegetable dealers.

A feeling of constriction descended on me one morning as I was touching up the paintwork of the barge, which hugged the quay squatly near where a motor crane, its gears grinding, advanced and retreated with nets of tarred barrels at its claw. A man in shiny serge trousers, stringed at the knees, bawled instructions from under wide nostrils, spat, and screwed each spittle under the sole of his iron-shod boot as though he were trying to obliterate it from his memory. The dockside, fanged and strutted with steel girders in the pale fog, sprawled shadowy oblongs into the hawser-shortened distance, which rang hollowly with the monotonous splutter of blunt-nosed drills. The feeling of constriction remained with me all morning.

It was not lessened by Ella's occasional appearances on deck, the first time with a bucket of refuse, the second with some wrung-out smalls and a pail of muddied, soap-broken water, which she emptied over the side.

I suppose it had come down to this. Considering everything, I had good reasons for remaining where I was, waiting for something to break. But at the same time I had a strange feeling of having lost my identity. I had become part of a situation which seemed to protect me against another, less enviable one, *the* one in which

I would have been involved had I gone to the police. But the more I became involved in the small world of the barge, the more I felt myself robbed of my identity.

It has always been that way with me as far as I can remember. I am a rootless kind of man. Often I find myself anxious to become involved with other people, but I am no sooner involved than I wish to be free again. Ten years ago I walked out of a university one spring morning with a small overnight bag. I never returned. Since then I have worked when I needed money, because I felt like moving, because I had to break out of a situation in which, though the necessities of life were provided for me, I felt myself being crushed. Now on the barge I was beginning to feel the familiar urge to break with the present. I couldn't keep my eyes off the ships on the river, especially those which I knew would sail over the tropics into the southern hemisphere.

During the day I noticed Ella's attitude towards me was becoming more proprietary. She made a number of references to the future, all of which took me, my continued presence, for granted. She talked about divorce. I sat through it all quietly, without protest, eating mechanically or smoking one fag after another, and answering her in monosyllables. When I thought of the plumber awaiting trial, my need to be safely involved came on me like a sickness, but my primitive protest was all the louder for that need.

And then Ella's voice would come back: "It wouldn't take long, would it, Joe?"

"What?"

"The divorce!"

"I don't know, Ella. I don't know anything about these things."

"I'll find out in Glasgow. That's where we were married."

"Yes."

"It'll be all right," Ella said with conviction.

I looked at her then and for a moment, in an oblique way, I found myself wondering what the reason for her determination was. It seemed pointless, not quite serious.

Later in the afternoon she went ashore to buy food. After she left, I tried to read but found I couldn't. The atmosphere was still constricted and yellow, drawn in on all sides by the black spokes of the dock. Every now and again metal clinked against metal, and then sharply the noise of riveting began. I was depressed, vaguely annoyed. I missed Ella, but only in an indirect way. I was bored with her. When she was there I had good reason to be bored, but when she was not I could only find the reason in myself, reflected in the fog and in the hawsers. I had a need to act which I repressed again and again. I wanted to break through the immobility in which I had become involved, but I had come to identify my safety with inaction, almost with the boredom which I was beginning to feel in relation to Ella.

But it couldn't go on. I had already decided to leave, I suppose, even that afternoon when I found myself telling myself not to be a fool, to wait and see, and I threw away a newly-lit cigarette and went below again.

When Ella returned, I was lying on the bunk. She was excited. She said immediately that the date of the plumber's trial had been set. I took the paper from her and glanced at it:

FATHER OF TWO TO STAND TRIAL
45-Year-Old Glasgow Man is Accused in Clyde Murder

There followed a brief account of the facts which the police had made public. Daniel Goon was known to have been intimate with the murdered woman, to have been associating with her for some time.

I did not need to read any further. I remembered Cathie talking very quietly, persuasively, after we had made love, telling me she was pregnant, that I was the father, and asking me to marry her. That was how it happened, with her running after me as I walked away. And, of course, she *had* told someone, a friend at work probably, and she had told that friend what was probably the truth, that the father was Goon. I was reading on and then Ella said that she thought it was four he had, children she meant, and I said yes, I had thought so too but that it had probably been a mistake. She began to empty the contents of the shopping bag on the table.

"Move your paper," she said. "You're in the way."

She stuffed a biscuit into her mouth.

I watched her chewing. Her teeth were large. They broke it to powder.

Later, her face was damp. She had been working at the hot stove.

I was still the hired man. She laughed as she paid me, colouring slightly, as though she weren't sure what service she paid me for.

"We're making good money," she said sometimes.

She included me, defending herself against her suspicions.

I made love to her under a haystack, noticing for the first time the tiny red network at the surface of her left thigh.

We moved along the canal. I saw the tramp, or it might have been another one, only this time he watched us from under the brim of his hat as we passed. When everything would be "good and proper…" She meant marriage, of course. The impropriety worried her. She wasn't sure of me. She talked about the divorce. Leslie wrote about it, almost apologetically. He hoped we were all well. He had a job as a night watchman in a warehouse. He asked how Jim was.

Sometimes I looked at her back. Her hips seemed broader. The apron string still dangled. Most of the time she tried to be attractive, wore lipstick, crossed her legs casually so that I could see the smooth white rise of the back of her thighs. In the dark we were still lovers. But during the day, I was conscious of her looking at me, analysing, speculating. Once she said she was looking forward to

Jim's growing up. Things would be easier on the barge then, *with the three of us*. It didn't seem to occur to her that I might object to the idea of living by proxy through her moronic child. I found it difficult to take her seriously. I felt her suspicion.

From the newspapers I derived the impression that they were going to find Goon guilty. We heard that Leslie alone would be required as a witness at the trial. I began to wonder whether I would find myself in the courtroom watching the web of guilt being woven round the wrong man. Ella joked about my sudden interest in the affair. She said she thought I wasn't interested in that kind of thing. But she was pleased at the same time. She helped me to cut out all the items from the different papers. Some evenings by the light of the oil lamp I sat with all the cuttings spread out on the table in front of me like a pack of cards in front of a fortune-teller.

What if they convicted him? I resented my connection with Goon. There *was* no murder. The guilt was invented. And then, with the question unanswered, I put my hand on Ella's belly, and as she turned towards me and I felt our thighs touch I had an impulse to abandon myself and my freedom to the sheer physical power of the woman whose hands were cupped over my buttocks and who thrust her abdomen towards me, to place myself at her mercy quietly with words there in the bed as the violence of our sensations increased, but each time before I spoke the orgasm was over and she was separate again, heavy and separate and dangerous. Conscious of the heat of her body close to me, so slack now and so dangerous, I lay awake for a long time. My mind was not blank but I could not have been said to be thinking of anything.

It was about this time that Ella picked up a letter from the post office. It was from her step-sister in Leith and had been lying in the post office for some time. Her husband had fallen off his lorry and been crushed to death by a bus. He was already buried. Gwendoline said that although she would be the first to admit that poor Sam and she didn't get on very well, it had come as a shock, a blow, in fact, which was not entirely countered by the damages she received from the company he worked for. She wanted to know when Ella would be in Leith.

It was Saturday. We were tied up in Glasgow. Ella sent Gwendoline a telegram to say that we would all come by train to visit her. In the compartment I sat beside Ella, and the kid, in a blue sailor suit and a sailor hat with a ribbon on it, sat opposite. I was feeling uncomfortable in a hard collar which she insisted I wear, and Ella was wearing a shiny black dress which was too tight for her and which made her look hot and red. We didn't talk much during the journey.

Gwendoline lived in a tenement which was just like any other tenement in Leith, a blackish-grey building, scaled on the inside by a creeping grey stair with an iron banister, leading to brown doors with brass plates on them at every landing. It smelled of refuse and decaying food. Hers was at the top of the building on the fifth floor. Jim was up first and waiting for us on the landing.

Gwendoline was in her dressing gown when she opened the door. It fell open at her breasts, which were long and white and pulpy like the long slender part of pears. She was younger than Ella. When she saw me, she caught up the dressing gown at her throat and smiled.

"This your new boyfriend, El?"

Ella sniffed.

"This is Joe," she said. "We're going to be married."

It sounded like an ultimatum, and she spoke it in an intense hard way, almost as though she were afraid she would be contradicted.

Gwendoline must have noticed my reaction because she laughed and said: "Pleased to meet you, Joe," and she stood away from the door to allow us to enter. "You'll excuse me not being dressed," she continued, "but I wasn't expecting gentlemen visitors." She ruffled Jim's hair as, eel-like, he slithered under my arm into the house.

Her lips were lipsticked heavily and her skin was very white, slightly yellowish in comparison, her mouth like a blood splash on porcelain. She led us into a sort of bed-sitting-room with an unmade bed and her clothes lying about. The window on the far side of the room wasn't open, the fire in the grate was out, and the air was sour, stuffy and motionless, impregnated with the cloying heat of a one-bar electric fire. It occurred to me that she had just got out of the bed to open the door.

"Sit down while I tidy up a bit," she said.

Ella looked around disapprovingly. This kind of thing brought out the worst in her.

Gwendoline was moving about stuffing things out of sight, her long chestnut hair was hanging in strings at her pallid cheeks. She smoked heavily. There were cigarette stubs everywhere and the first two fingers of her right hand were nicotine-stained at the nails.

At first, I didn't pay much attention to her. I was looking at Ella. She sat in her shiny black dress in an old armchair and her lips were pursed and an aura of respectability emanated from her. It seemed to move up from her stiff haunches to the tilt of her neck; a moral judgement smelling of eau-de-Cologne. I wondered how near I had come to committing suicide when I almost told her the truth about Cathie. I was horrified to think that I had nearly spoken. It seemed absurd now. I looked away from her at a little spark on the element of the electric fire. Zzz... Leaning close I could hear it sizzle. A sudden feeling like a dull hammer blow, Goon's mouth opened in a wide scream, the hairs of his purple head alive with shock... thank God they didn't electrocute them...

I was in the way.

"Excuse me, Joe!" Gwendoline said as she brushed past me. She had taken her hand away from the top of the dressing gown and, as she stooped to lift a silk stocking from the floor, I saw the breasts hanging, long and pear-shaped, and they glowed with an orange

115

colour where the electric fire was reflected on them. "I'll make you all a cup of tea," she said as she stood up again.

Ella said she would help her, and the two women, followed by the kid, went through to the next room. I glanced at the cigarette butts and the soiled underclothing pushed hurriedly out of sight under a cushion, and then I walked over to the bed again and put my hand on the sheet where she had lain. It was still warm and there was a feel of biscuit crumbs under my fingers. On the bedside table was a bent hairpin, a piece of ribbon, an ashtray with red-tipped fag ends, and a little grey ball of chewing gum. Lying beside the ashtray was a bottle of aspirin. Like an inventory clerk, I took stock. Gwendoline, a widow. There was something unpurposeful about Gwendoline, a sort of tadpole quality which suggested that if she found herself in bed with a man she would stay there because she was too lazy to get out. At the foot of the bed there was a morning newspaper and a book on astrology. In the latter, as it fell open in my hands, I saw she had underlined the following:

The terror which the moon inspires in us is not altogether unjustified. The proofs of its evil influence are corroborated by a hundred flagrant facts. A red moon is particularly detestable.

I puzzled over that for some time before I shut the book and returned with the newspaper to my chair.

There was nothing in it about my crime.

I was sitting there when they returned with the tea.

"Gwen's having a holiday with us," Ella said almost immediately.

"Oh?"

"She's coming on the barge for a week or two."

Gwendoline smiled at me. She had gathered her dressing gown properly about her now and secured it, her tapering breasts out of sight.

"I hope you don't mind, Joe? I don't suppose I'm breaking up a honeymoon or anything?"

I shrugged my shoulders. I was glad that Ella spoke before I could say anything because I could not think of anything to say.

"It'll be good for her," Ella said. "She's going to pack now and come back with us on the train tonight."

"I'll just have a cup of tea," Gwendoline said.

Two days later, on a fine spring morning, we loaded early with limestone. We were well along the canal by midday.

It was good to be standing there at the wheel with the flat green and brown fields stretching on either side as far as the horizon. At that point the landscape was almost treeless and the view across the fields was uninterrupted. The sun was strong and the yellow-black canal water reacted to it, glowing behind us as it peeled off the bilges in long black flakes. The wheel was warm with the sun. Everything seemed far away, events as well as things, and I almost forgot the plumber and the dead woman and Leslie and even the two women who were below.

Gwendoline did not get up for breakfast. She slept late – for her complexion. She was not the kind of woman who could make herself useful on the barge, not that I wanted her to do that. I was not interested in getting anything done quickly or efficiently. I should have been quite content to stop the engine and moor along the bank somewhere, or to tie up for a week until the weather broke or until we ran out of food. Not quite true perhaps. Ordinarily I could have said that without misgivings. That was the way I lived. But since the arrest of the plumber I was uneasy, idiotically anchored to time, to events and processes over which I had no control.

She came on deck around noon, up through the companionway and close to me almost before I was aware of her. She had done her face up. After watching me for a few minutes, she wanted to take the wheel, so I sat down near her as she steered. I rolled a cigarette.

. first, neither of us spoke. She appeared to be engrossed in her work, which she did well (she had been brought up on the barge with Ella) and she was looking straight ahead. And then she put a question to me.

"Are you really going to marry Ella, Joe?"

"That's what she said," I said non-committally.

"What about you?" she said.

"I don't say anything."

"Oh, have it your own way!" she said. "It's none of my business."

I agreed with her. She looked back along the canal.

She was wearing slacks. She had brushed the stringy appearance out of her hair, but its auburn colour made her face appear very white, like bread and jam because of the sudden lipstick. She was not as tall as Ella, younger, thinner. She was intelligent enough to know that I had no intention of marrying Ella, but it did not seem to worry her.

She looked, I thought then, as though she had just got out of bed. She would always look like that. Even in the spring sunshine she had that damp white look about her which some women have, so that you think that if you brushed the palm of your hand over their skin it would come away quite wet, the kind of pallor which makes you think of sickrooms and flannel underwear. It occurred to me that she would probably have T.B. The thought of her slender breasts seemed to confirm the impression. She would be white all over, white with a few pink parts where she had sat down or where her belt chafed, a long white root with a tuft of brittle auburn fuzz at the centre. And yet there was something attractive about Gwendoline, not in her features, which were flat and puttylike, not in the forward jut of her abdomen nor in the premature thinness of her legs, but in her whole attitude. I doubted whether she had ever felt righteous.

I had finished rolling my cigarette and I struck a match on the sole of my boot. I threw the match over the stern and watched it heaved aside on the surface of the water, and its movement reminded me of that of the bottle and the matchbox and the spar of wood which had moved past beneath me as I searched for Cathie's body in the water.

Gwendoline was speaking again.

"Don't you ever get bored with the canal, Joe?"

"Sure I do, sometimes."

"I thought you would. You don't look the type."

I didn't contradict her.

"You've got to be born to it," she said.

I flicked the ash from my cigarette in reply.

"And even then," she continued, "if you're like me you don't want any part of it."

"Why not?"

"It's no life," she said. "I could tell the first time I saw you you weren't cut out for it."

I was not impressed by her assurance.

"Did you see it in the stars?" I said mockingly.

"You're ignorant," she said flatly. "And you're not funny."

We heard the kid scream down below.

"He's a brat," Gwendoline said. "But seriously, Joe, you know as well as I do that you're fed up with it."

"It's a job like any other."

She laughed at that.

"When are you going to walk out on her, Joe?"

"Today, tomorrow, the next day," I said. "I can't read the stars."

"Stuff it!" Gwendoline said rudely.

After a few moments silence, we talked on. She was telling me that Ella didn't drink and that she couldn't understand a person who didn't drink, and that if it were not for the head she had in the morning she herself would get drunk every night. She liked gin, she said, not gin and lime or gin and vermouth or anything else; gin straight. She didn't find it bitter. She suggested we ought to go

119

for a drink together some time, that we could tell Ella that we were going to the cinema, not that we would, she didn't suppose I liked the cinema any more than she did. To pass the time, what she liked was good game of nap and a spot of gin.

In spite of her slacks, she looked incongruous at the wheel. The slacks were of a soft green velours, grease-stained and with bags at the knees. She was not wearing stockings. She told me that if there was one thing she hated it was to go to the dentist's.

Ella came on deck a short time afterwards and called Gwendoline to go and eat. We usually had dinner in shifts like that while we were under way. I was left alone on deck. I could hear the two women talking and laughing below, and then the kid's voice, coarsely sibilant, and I found myself envying them all suddenly. In one way, and for each of them, they were secure; the absurdity which touched them (if at all) was an acceptable one; they were protected by the structures of their own minds, by the fact that they were neither implicated in "murder" nor, to ordinary thinking, "insane". But the absurdity which threatened me was the end of all possibility, and often when I was alone I experienced a terrible certainty that it would strike and that when it did I should be free neither to accept nor to reject it. There was nothing un-final about death. No sane man could accept it.

But I was glad to be alone there at the wheel again with the sun on my hands and the water ahead pointing at distance like a javelin shaft along which crept towards me a horse-drawn barge, the Clydesdale straining forwards and sideways with a man at its head. For a long time it remained in the distance, a man, horse, and barge, like an insect with three segments to its body, and then, all at once, they were separate and growing in size more rapidly until finally they were near and abreast and the man was waving his hand in greeting. Neither of us spoke. When they had passed, I turned round, and the horse still leant forwards and sideways with a man at its head and the man was looking straight ahead. The voices from below came back to me again. The kid was saying something about rice pudding and Ella had raised her voice. Apart from a slight apprehensiveness, I had no qualms about Ella. She had become again just what she was at the beginning, Leslie's wife. Sooner or later – I was temporarily unable to make any decision – I would leave her. I was conscious of her almost as a chemical reaction which was trying to assimilate me. She was trying to force me to give what I had given freely. I think Gwendoline knew that from the beginning and that she sympathized with me, and perhaps that was what attracted me about her.

We tied up at Clowes in the middle of the afternoon. Ella had wanted to go on for a bit because it would be light until after seven, but she didn't insist. Gwendoline had already told her that she wanted me to take her to the cinema.

Gwendoline was young and old. She was less sensitive than Ella and it was obvious that she despised her. And I could see that she wanted me to be unfaithful to Ella with her. It was difficult to believe that she was only twenty-nine. She looked old and yet her body gave the impression sometimes of being almost adolescent. She had changed into a red skirt and a green jumper the front of which, decorated with white vees, dragged flatly because she wore nothing to support her long conical breasts. Her shoes were white court-shoes, toeless, and when she crossed her legs I was fascinated by the thick varnish-red toenail at the point of each and by the fine coppery hairs which ran down her shins in twin spines. I wondered vaguely if she was a prostitute. I could sense that she was really indifferent to men, only vaguely sexual.

A bow of lipstick was revealed brightly on the rim of her teacup.

We did not talk much on the way to the pub (the hotel bar, the only one in which women were allowed) and, seated at the table,

red, green, white and thin, Gwendoline smoked one cigarette after
another and sipped her gin. She dabbed her lips with a handkerchief
and said she thought it was about time Ella took a jump to herself.

"Get us another gin, Joe," she said.

I had paid for the first drinks with the change I had in my pocket.
As I drew out my wallet to pay for the new drinks, a photograph of
Cathie fell out of it on to the floor. I froze momentarily. The waitress
picked it up and handed it to me without looking at it. As calmly as
possible, I returned it to my wallet. Gwendoline was smiling.

"An old girlfriend?" she said.

"Yes," I replied. "She died."

"But you still carry it?"

"I don't know why. I ought to have destroyed it a long time ago."

"Of course you should! The dead can look after themselves!"

She screwed her cigarette into the ashtray.

"Drink up," she said. "We've got business to attend to."

We made love very coldly and mechanically in a field. Not exactly
business, because no money passed between us. It was very dark,
the ground for the most part firm but in places, where the wind had
caused a crust to form on the mud, soft as our feet sank in. Her
cheeks were very cold. When I touched her breasts she did not react
at all. The glow of her cigarette was bright and dim evenly; she
seemed to be completely abstracted.

She interrupted me. She said she didn't want any trouble. And
then, when it was over, and she got up she complained that I had
got her all messed up and she spent a long time tidying herself. It
was over quickly. Her cigarette was still smouldering in the grass. I
put my foot on it. I was wondering whether she always made love in
that way. She had scarcely been aware of me.

We walked slowly back to the barge talking in a desultory way
about Leith, where we had both lived. She liked Leith, she said,
and she thought she would go back there and settle down when the

122

damages came for her husband's death. It was hard to believe he was dead, she said. What convinced her more than anything else was the fact that she was no longer wakened early in the morning by his boots clumping in and out from the room to the kitchen. He was a big man, as big as Leslie. She laughed then. Poor Sam. It was too bad the way she talked about him, she knew that, but what was the use of telling lies? Of course, she was sorry for him, so sudden it was, to go to your work one morning like any other and then suddenly to have it happen like that. It made you think. It gave her a queer turn when they brought her the news. Luckily, she hadn't time to dwell on it. He had to be buried – as soon as possible on account of how the bus had run over him when he fell from his lorry. The police were very helpful, especially one fair-headed young man with a walrus moustache who kept making her cups of tea. She had always disliked the police, but it just went to show some of them were human beings too.

It was a quiet funeral and the young policeman took her home afterwards and she felt sorry for him, he was so clumsy, so she let him do it to her on the couch. Somehow the bed would not have seemed right. He was very nervous and it was a long time before he could bring himself to do it. He said he felt like he was desecrating the grave. The funeral had taken all the spunk out of him. But when she said now or never, he opened up and disclosed his fright. Well, that was all right as far as that went but she thought it was a bit thick when he kept calling on her, bringing her violets and lilies of the valley every day when he was off duty. She gave him an inch and he took a mile, she said. I had the impression that she expected me to reply and so I nodded and said that although I could understand the young policeman's desire to continue the relationship I could understand her point of view too.

"I should hope so," she said rather pertly. She said that she had found most men were like that and that she hoped I wasn't.

I assured her that I wasn't.

She was glad of that.

She became more confidential. Anyway, she said, it was not what it was cracked up to be. She knew that and she was sure I did. All that Hollywood bunk, she said. She'd take a glass of gin for preference any time, and, by an association of ideas she came to the conclusion that you got nothing for nothing in this life.

I said that I supposed she was right.

"You're smart, Joe," she said. "I could see that the moment you walked in. Now Ella's a bloody fool. She always was."

Looking down, I could see her feet walking slowly over the stones, and above them the thin white legs to the level of her skirt. She was smoking. She seemed to assume that I felt like her about everything. She did not expect to be contradicted.

I asked her how she came to leave the barge in the first place.

That was not where she had made her mistake, she said. It was no life on the barge. Her big mistake was getting married, Sam giving her two pounds a week to run the house and expecting her to be a bloody skivvy for him. She asked me if I would credit it.

I nodded sympathetically.

She could have earned more every night of the week, she went on, and not running around picking up things after any man. It hadn't taken her long to realize her mistake and after that she did the best she could, but it was difficult with Sam coming home in the evening and you had to make do with what you could get, which wasn't much because all the young men were working and that left only the old-age pensioners and those who were on the dole and neither kind had much money. Still, it wasn't so bad because the pensioners didn't ask for much, just a feel usually, over in a minute, not like Sam.

We were coming near the barge and she said we'd better pretend to Ella that we'd been to the cinema and so we agreed on a film which we'd both seen so that we would be able to speak about it if she asked.

"If all men were like you, Joe," Gwendoline said, "perhaps things would be different."

I wasn't quite sure I knew what she meant but I didn't contradict her Whatever she said, she had a tone of hard conviction, and I didn't want to make an enemy of her.

Ella was very quiet. She made tea for us. Gwendoline looked at me and made a face.

I was wondering if Ella suspected about Gwendoline and me. She had avoided my eye ever since we returned and it seemed to me she had a hurt look, but she didn't question us.

Gwendoline was smiling. I noticed that her little finger was cocked like a trigger as she lifted her cup to drink. I was annoyed with her. She was merely making things difficult. She appeared to take pleasure in seeing Ella subdued and me without words, not knowing how to make conversation.

About half an hour later Gwendoline went to bed in the forward cabin. As soon as she had gone Ella prepared to go to bed. She looked tired. She cleared the table and began to undress, still without speaking. I went over to her and tried to take her in my arms but she pushed me away.

"Leave me alone, Joe."

I thought, "To hell with them both." I went up on deck and smoked a cigarette. It was a clear night. The stars were very high and far away, the sky vaulted, dark and impersonal, and I knew that under the same impersonal sky were other men who, in spite of the fact that in a few day's time the plumber, Goon, would stand trial, would be weighing the evidence, searching in a routine way for a new clue. Yet the night was motionless, empty. I thought of Ella. I knew now that I was going to leave. And sooner or later I would have to go far away. I remained on deck for half an hour, smoking. When I went down again Ella was asleep.

4

F ROM WHERE I SAT AT THE TABLE in the bar I could see the oblong of
glass on which "Bass" was readable in reverse, the last daylight
merging above the partition with the pale electric light which had
perceptibly grown in intensity as daylight faded, becoming yellower,
more in keeping with the men in the bar, with the bottles and with
the conversation, the scene seeming somehow more in focus in artificial light; and from outside beyond the swing doors the clang of city
traffic moved inwards with the man who hesitated there, his pink
gaze floating over the crowd in attempted recognition, until the gaze
arrested and his hand raised in greeting – Bill! – and the other turning from a group and smiling in cross-recognition, the swing doors
pivoted and steadied, then closed, cutting off outside noises and
restoring volume and excitement to the conversation, drink calls,
bar sounds, of which I had been conscious during the time I had sat
there, acutely conscious as a man tends to be when for one reason or
another he is excluded. I had laid down the newspaper, not knowing whether or not to be satisfied that Goon would stand trial in ten
days' time and I had glanced at the fading panel of the daylight and
sipped the froth from my beer, tasting malt. I had heard his name
mentioned angrily by one man who wanted to know why we wasted
public money giving the bastard a trial, at least one other saying
"Hear, hear," and another with a grin making some remark which
caused himself and the man next to him to guffaw. The conversation swayed from heavy to light, interrupted occasionally by a stac-
cato demand for a drink and by someone flourishing a newspaper. I
glanced down at my own newspaper and in a side column read: "'If

he did it, he'd be better off dead,' wife says." That for poor Goon. Poor bastard to be married to a woman like that. I shuddered. At the bar a suggestion that Goon might not be guilty was greeted by a solid protesting wall of disbelief until the speaker, asking them to mark his words, said it was obviously the work of a homicidal maniac, a Jack the Ripper who didn't use razors.

"Necrophilia, it's called, but they won't let it out," he said in the ensuing silence. "Mark my words! You'll see!"

The conversation grew more heated. I overheard one man say hanging was too good for a man like Goon; a man who couldn't let women alone ought to be burned.

I was isolated from it all by my certain knowledge of Goon's innocence and I began to have foreknowledge of what a fantastic puppet play the trial would turn out to be. That disturbed me, and the glare from the yellow-painted wall was making my eyes smart, that and the excessive smoke. I had been looking at the wall, listening with my ears only… somehow that made it all less real. But I didn't stay long. I emptied my glass and left the bar with the wife's words ringing in my ears: *If he did it, he'd be better off dead…*

Jesus Christ!

I walked back to the barge. It was tied up quite close to where we had fished Cathie's body from the water. I found myself wondering where she was now. She would be buried in some cemetery or other. I wondered whether they had a special place for people who had been murdered and whose relatives didn't claim them, an anonymous pit into which their scarred and post-autoptic remains were gradually fed. I was stopped by the violence of my thoughts. I felt empty and very alone, as though in some anomalous way it was part of myself which had been labelled, boxed, and interred. And I resented the prurient interest of the men at the bar.

As I walked I remembered very well how different her body was from either Ella's or Gwendoline's. It was younger, smoother, with no flatulence; a brown-yellow becoming yellow-white on the underside; and I remembered being soothed out of tedious wakefulness in her soft arms.

There was a time, I suppose, when we were happy. Long summer days in the cottage at the edge of the moor when we saw nobody. And I was going to write a book, a masterpiece, and we would go abroad. We spent the few hundred pounds that came to her when her father died. For a few weeks after that I did odd jobs about the neighbouring farms. But it couldn't last. "If I see another bloody potato I'll go stark raving mad!" So we moved to town and Cathie got a job. She came home tired and after a while there was an undercurrent of bitterness. "I wouldn't mind so much if I thought you were ever going to finish it," she said. "Do you think it's easy? Do you think all I have to do is to sit down and write the bloody thing? I don't have a plot. I don't have characters. I'm not interested in all the usual paraphernalia. Don't you understand? That's literature, false. I've got to start with the here and now. I..." "No, I don't understand," she replied. "I don't know why you can't write an ordinary book, one other people will understand. It's been eight months now. I get up early in the morning, sit in a lousy office all day, and when I come home you're either drunk or asleep! What have you done today, Joe, while I was out earning the money for us to eat with?" "I made some custard," I said dangerously. "You did what?" "I made some custard. Here it is." I held up a large bowl of rich yellow custard. That morning when I found myself unable to work I looked round for something to do. I found an old recipe for custard. It was the best custard I had ever tasted. I was looking forward to Cathie's coming home so that she could taste it. "Custard!" she said as she might have said "Bedbugs!" "I work all day and you make custard!" Without saying anything she began to change her clothes.

"About the custard," I said after a moment, "it struck me as a good idea. So I made it. Here it is over on the dresser."

I walked towards the bowl. It was a very large bowl and it must have contained about two and a half pints of custard.

"I don't give a damn where it is!" she said, pulling off one of her stockings, "You'll have to eat it yourself, that's all. I certainly don't want any custard."

I looked at her. Suddenly I was annoyed with her. I had been bored all day. I had enjoyed making the custard. I was damned if I was going to have her sit there making nasty remarks about my custard. Her face had taken on that kind of stupidly defiant look. It angered me. She was not looking at me even. She was straightening the seams of her stockings. Above them were her black nylon panties. That was all she was wearing. Her hair, still in cattails after her work, was hanging over her face as she bent to twist the stocking straight about her calf. I spoke slowly and threateningly.

"I made the custard and you're going to eat it," I said.

I don't know why I wanted her to eat it but I did.

"You know what you can do with it!" she said derisively.

"I know what I am going to do with it!" I replied.

I threw it at her.

The custard, slipping from the bowl, a massive yellow gobbet of it, sailed across the room and struck her on the breasts. It had not hardened. It had the consistency of a soft glue paste. She screamed and tilted backward in her chair so that her body, now covered with custard, sprawled across the dusty oilcloth on the floor. Her thighs meanwhile in their upward arc as the chair spun backward and her hot spread buttocks glimmering whitely beneath the gauze-fine nylon stimulated me to further action. I lifted a stick from the fireplace, the split side of an egg crate, and leapt upon her. She was whimpering with fright.

"You bastard! you bastard! you bastard!" she was saying.

I grasped her by one arm, twisted her about so that her great big and now custard smeared buttocks were facing me and with

all the strength of my right arm I thrashed at them w̱
slat of wood. I thrashed her mercilessly for about a mı.
was making shrill whinnying noises as she threshed about c
dusty floor. The custard was dripping off her nipples and mingḻ.
already with the short hairs of her sex. I paused, moved over to
the mantelpiece and grasped a bottle of bright blue ink. She was
seated on her haunches, crying, wheezing and shaking. I emptied
the contents of the bottle over her head so that it ran through her
hair and down over her face and shoulders where it met the custard.
It was then that I remembered the sauce and the vanilla essence. I
stirred them into the mixture, tomato ketchup, brown sauce, and
a bottle of vanilla essence, blues, greens, yellows, and reds, all the
colours of the rainbow.

I don't know whether she was crying or laughing as I poured a
two-pound bag of sugar over her. Her whole near-naked body was
twitching convulsively, a blue breast and a yellow-and-red one, a
green belly, and all the odour of her pain and sweat and gnashing.
By that time I was hard. I stripped off my clothes, grasped the slat
of the egg crate, and moved among her with prick and stick, like a
tycoon.

When I rose from her, she was a hideous mess, almost unrecognizable as a white woman, and the custard and the ink and
the sugar sparked like surprising meats on the haired twist of her
satisfied mound.

I washed and went out without a word. When I returned, there
was no evidence of the mess. She was in bed, and as I got in beside
her, I felt her arms close about me and she kissed me on the lips.

It was a painful memory now. Not long after that we broke up,
quietly, with no hysterics. "You should have been rich, Joe," she
said to me. "It might have worked then. I loved you." Past tense.
Because I was not rich I should submit to the harness? "Ah, but
'twas my fearless rebel eye that made you love me, dear?…"

I was so engrossed in my thoughts that I almost turned directly into the street where the café was, where she and I had sat on the night of her death. As I turned the corner, a sense of familiarity made me halt and I stood for a moment wondering until the fact of my foolishness struck me and then I turned and walked quickly back the way I had come.

When I returned to the barge Gwendoline was sitting alone in the cabin reading a paper. The kid was asleep in the for'ard cabin. As I came down through the companionway she looked up.

"When's your birthday, Joe?"

"What?"

"Your horoscope," she said. "I'll read it to you."

"Where's Ella?"

She laughed.

"El's gone daft! Come on and sit down."

She poured me a glass of gin from the bottle in front of her.

"What do you mean 'daft'?"

"She's gone to see Leslie."

I sat down, accepting the glass she offered me, and drank. It wasn't until the bitter taste of the gin stung my palate and my throat that I remembered that I hated raw gin.

"What I can't imagine," Gwendoline said, "is what she wants with a man like that."

"He's a rock," I said, getting up. I didn't listen to her reply. I was collecting my various personal possessions and stowing them into a small kitbag with which I came to the barge.

"What d'you think you're doing?" Gwendoline demanded.

"I'm clearing out," I said. "I should have gone a long time ago."

Gwendoline went into a fit of hysterical laughter. Her white face with her vivid thin lips was like a ghoul's in the light from the oil lamp.

"Have you seen my mirror?" I said.

"What mirror?"

"It's a metal one. I use it for shaving. It's got a hole in the top end."

"Are you really going off tonight?"

"Yes."

"Have a last drink then."

"No. I hate the stuff."

I found the mirror in the table drawer and put it beside the rest of my property in the kitbag.

"Aw, come on! Have a drink!"

"I don't like raw gin."

She looked at me for a moment and then burst into laughter again. I looked at her. She sat with her elbows on the table, laughing hysterically, her face pale and her coppery red hair like a wig in the lamplight.

"You burn that photograph yet?"

I froze, and found myself sitting down. "What photograph?"

"Aw, you know!" Her voice was growing thicker with the gin. "The one of your ole girfrien'."

"Oh, that one. Sure, I burned it."

"Thash good. Don't like souveneers, heh, heh, no regrets, Joe, old boy, whadiyou shay?"

I poured myself a small shot of gin and clinked glasses with her." Let the dead bury the dead," I said.

"Thash my Joe!" She slumped forward on the table and I stared for a moment at the scrawny neck where the dark roots of her hair showed, the glint of iron filings.

She hadn't seen the photograph. I was reasonably certain of that. And I *had* burned it since. Anyway, I had to take the chance. I couldn't imagine myself killing her. Kill the old Italian in the café too! I got up and climbed up through the companionway.

Outside on the quay I looked around at the distant flickering lights and then walked away into the city.

Part Three

1

DURING THE NIGHT I listened to the plumbing. The bed was hard and the broken state of the springs made the mattress uneven. The one-room-and-kitchen flat was at the front of the house and the windows gave on to the street, a narrow crescent-shaped street, the pavement of which on the opposite side was on four levels, lava-like steps which sloped downwards on to a narrow bed of cobbles along which only three vehicles ever came – the dust cart, the coal cart and the milk-lorry. The street was lit by five lamps, four lamp posts and one scrolled Victorian bracket riveted almost opposite the window to the crumbling grey wall opposite. And now the light from it filtered into the room where I was lying, in the recess bed in the kitchen, and gleamed dully on the bone-like rim of the sink from whose pipes the plopping and gurgling sounds came, and cast the floor in shadows so that the bits of furniture seemed to be suspended in mid-air and I had the impression that I was within a shaft with unsubstantial furniture around me, and that below, where no floor was, the shaft continued downwards without sensible bottom.

I was lying on my side, and with my hand I reached downwards tentatively and touched the oilcloth on the floor. The feel of it reassured me and I caressed it with the backs of my fingers. My head rested at the edge of the bed and I tried to make out with my eyes the surface which my fingers touched. A moment later it was there, shadowy, under the dull droop-white of my fingers.

The noise from the pipes approached and retreated like a train along the rails. Out of the corner of my eye, beyond the hanging window, I could see the coloured contours of the lamp bracket and the pale glow which it cast above the nameplate of the street. If I had not known the name already I would have been unable to decipher it from that distance and in that light, but as it was I could see it, blurred at first and then in sharp focus, as though I were its creator. It was called Lucien Street. It was adjacent to Black Street.

I turned back to the woman beside me and laid my hand on her belly just above her pelvis. She was sleeping soundly and rather noisily. My fingers moved down softly, exploring the intricacy of her dormant being. It was the night before the day on which Goon was to stand trial. I was unable to sleep.

In the small Bridgeton flat I understood from the beginning that it would be possible as the lodger to avail myself of the narrow-breasted, knuckle-haunched, thin blonde of twenty-five whose husband worked as a night-watchman in a warehouse in Stockwell Street, there being only a flimsy door which would not close properly between the kitchen where they slept, the two children in a cot and the wife in a cavity bed, and the small room which was mine.

The door from the stairs opened into the kitchen.

Her husband's first act when he came in at daybreak was to remove his boots. These were big boots, warped by the sweat of his feet and shod heavily with iron.

His next act was to make tea for the adults in bed. At the same time he resuscitated the dead embers of the fire and warmed his feet.

Before he retired I got up from my bed in the small room, to which I had retreated a couple of hours before, and went through to the kitchen to shave myself at the sink. While I was shaving I heard the woman gasp suddenly as the man joined her. He did so with no gentleness, taking what was his.

I didn't look around. I watched the soap thicken on the end of my shaving brush and remembered how from the beginning she had unquestioningly but without passion accepted my own embraces.

I remained tinkering with my shaving kit, washing one piece after another under the tap, the soap swirling from amongst the bristles of the brush until the grunts of the man and the heavy breathing of the woman were over. I turned to the man, who was lying sideways across his wife, and said I was going to watch the trial of Goon that day, that it would be interesting. He nodded sleepily.

In spite of the mute rivalry which existed between us over the woman who – he must have known – served us both, there was also a tacit understanding. We were friends and we drank together, that too almost from the beginning – the night on which I had left the barge I met him in a pub – when, back in the kitchen, he said: "Your kip's in the other room. If there's anything you need, the wife here'll attend to you." The wife, a thin, hard-muscled woman of the slums, cocked an eyebrow and looked me up and down. Under her look I felt the courage drain away from my spine and I could think of nothing better to do than to produce a handful of half-crowns and shillings and pay two weeks' rent in advance, laying the money, as though I were buying her, at the corner of the table near the wife who, after a moment's hesitation, passed two of the coins over to the husband and swept the remainder into the pocket of her apron. The man accepted them without expression and invited me to go downstairs for a drink.

"See you're not late for work," his wife said as we went out.

Over a beer we talked about her. All the time I felt it was strange he didn't talk about her body, nor even about the woman really, only, and with a stubborn primitive knowledge of what he was talking about, about his experience of her.

At the corner of the street we parted company, he to go to the warehouse, I to return to the flat. For a moment he seemed reluctant to go.

And then, when he was gone, and with the weight of chains at my abdomen, I was on my way back to her and the tiny flat in

Lucien Street. I paused on Black Street, the scene of *my* crime. It was when I entered the flat again that she said without formality that she supposed I'd be like the last. She said it without warmth and added: "Wait till the wains go to sleep."

She dressed in front of the fire without looking at me. I finished my own activities at the sink and then sat down in front of the fire and smoked a cigarette. She was frying bacon. A moment later she broke two eggs into the pan, let them fry for a moment, and then emptied the entire contents of the pan on to a plate which she thrust at me. I took it to the table with a knife and fork, broke some bread and commenced to eat. A moment later she laid a cup of strong tea beside me.

"You going to that police court later on?"

I nodded.

"You think that Goon's guilty?"

"They haven't established it was murder yet."

"What d'you mean?" Connie said.

"They haven't proved it was."

"Oh, they know that," she said vaguely, bringing her own plate with bacon only on to the table beside me. "A woman doesn't get undressed for nothing."

"That's not the point. So she made love."

"You'll see," Connie insisted. "They'll hang him, the poor bugger."

I was uneasy about it. I could not deny it was likely. But there was nothing I could do. I would go to the trial. Something might turn up. But after all the dramatic news coverage there had to be a victim. I would go. Leslie would be there, perhaps Ella. And Gwendoline? When I thought of her I became even more uneasy. She threatened more than my peace of mind. But she hadn't seen the photograph. I had it out of sight too quickly for that. I thought for a while that I would leave the city altogether, even go abroad, at once. But I had to go to the trial to see how the lawyers and other court functionaries committed legal murder. The image of Cathie's naked body floated before me, like Macbeth's dagger. But during the trial neither the victim nor the murderers would dream of taking their clothes off. Too bad. The thought was more than amusing. The judge would be an old man. He would lose all dignity if he were forced to perform without his majestic trappings. His skinniness, his obesity perhaps, would give the lie to the odour of righteousness. The crowd would laugh at his pomposity and shout down the brutality of his sentence. All judges, it occurred to me, all lawyers and lawyers' clerks ought to be forced to try their case in the nude. The naked truth. In this context it would be more than a metaphor. It was doubtful if they would be able to convict anyone. Their voices, reflecting the all-too-human evidence of the naked postures, would lack conviction.

I was out in the street early and found myself walking along Argyle Street in the general direction of the courts. I stopped for a cup of tea at a snack counter, smoked two or three cigarettes, and then continued on my way. As I walked through the town, a strange feeling of confidence settled upon me. The rain was on and then it was off. There were women in the street, typists, shop-girls, clerks, hurrying to work. Men in suits, in overalls, in uniforms. A shot of whisky, which I drank from a hipflask, appeared to have drawn things more clearly together. It gave me at the same time assurance, certainty, not *of* anything; confidence simply in the face of the necessity of my isolation.

I boarded a tram. As soon as I was seated I found myself putting my hand in my pocket to make sure that my money was still there. Of course it was. I smiled at the almost transparent reflection of myself in the window and saw beyond it, like a memory walking out of my head, a girl in a pink coat who stood looking in a shop window, a glimpse of legs which under the hem of the coat were pink and sunburned as Cathie's had been, and I wondered whether under different circumstances I would have had the courage to get off and introduce myself. The tram moved on, an island of windows. I got off with as little purpose as I had got on. The pavement was, if anything, even more crowded. People pushed past me to board the tram, women with parcels mostly, touchable, aware of me as an obstacle only. It occurred to me that normally speaking, in relation to other people, I could be regarded primarily as an obstacle.

When I reached the pavement I had already decided to have another shot of whisky. I made my way to a milk bar and walked through into the men's toilet. There, sitting on the lavatory seat, I allowed the whisky to trickle down my throat. I replaced the cap on the flask, pocketed it, and on second thoughts urinated. There was an excitement at my belly which made itself known at the surface in a slight sweat. I read the various invitations to sexual abnormality which covered the walls about me. A moment later, I arranged my clothes and walked directly out through the milk bar on to the street.

An old man with a grey beard and whitely congealed, sightless eyes was selling shoelaces and pencils. The shoelaces were draped over the arm which manipulated a white stick as a probe The pencils in a bunch were clutched in the other hand. The head nodded wisely. It occurred to me that he was probably a fool even before he was blind. A shilling for St. Francis. I skirted him, unwilling to be touched. I pulled on a pair of gloves and went into a post office.

I bought a letter-card. Over at the window, with one of the post office pens, I wrote the following message in block capitals:

I HAVE NO INTENTION OF SURRENDERING TO YOU NOR OF PROVIDING YOU WITH FURTHER INFORMATION. IF YOU CONDEMN GOON YOU WILL CONDEMN A MAN WHO KNOWS NOTHING OF THE CIRCUMSTANCES OF CATHERINE DIMLY'S DEATH. I ALONE WAS WITH HER AT THE TIME SHE

DIED. THE DROWNING WAS ACCIDENTAL. I CANNOT PROVE THIS WITHOUT
IDENTIFYING MYSELF AND WERE I TO DO SO I SUSPECT I WOULD STEP
STRAIGHT INTO HIS CONDEMNED BOOTS. I CAN'T TAKE THE RISK. BUT
GOON IS INNOCENT.

I waited for the ink to dry, not wishing to have the message appear on
the post office blotter, and then, sealing the letter-card, I addressed
it to the judge who was trying the case and dropped it in the box.

Of course I was under no illusion that my melodramatic message
would in any way affect the proceedings (Goon's wife might have
written it, or any practical joker), but however slight the possibility
of its being taken seriously it was worth the effort. To sow a seed of
doubt in the mind of the judge… I supposed it wouldn't even have
that effect. Whether or not they are conscious of it, all judges must
look upon themselves as God. To judge is to presume one is God.
That is why wise men put words forbidding us to judge one another
in the mouth of God.

A policeman directed me to the particular courtroom. It was
already quite crowded. Mostly middle-aged women. I had the
impression that I was watching a parliament of birds.

As soon as I was seated I began for some reason or another to
think of my shaving mirror. I remembered that on more than one
occasion I had dropped it and I was being continually surprised
by the fact that it didn't break. No matter how often I repeated
to myself that it was made of metal I could not rid myself of the
response of expectation that it would break. Why did I think of
that then?

I tried to make myself comfortable on the seat, looked closely
at the polished wood; my legs were tired, and that made me look
at the scarred black leather of my boots. In a way, I was bored, I
hadn't realized how utterly dependent on things I had become, even
if only to catalogue them, saying over and over again, the door,

the seat, the boots, the mirror, the thing to wash in; if I had had
a big ledger I could have drawn up an inventory of things, neatly
arranging the columns of the names of the microscopic objects,
which, with the courtroom about me, formed so large a part of my
experience. Then I might have progressed to microscopic objects.
With a ledger and a pencil I could have kept going indefinitely. The
seats, for example, were grouped rows, and they were really benches
with backs and multiple legs. The mirror – for some reason I had it
in my inside pocket – had four corners, the scarf of the woman next
to me was seen, when examined closely, to be composed of weaves
of wool ranging from a distinct red, through all the various shades
of purple, to one strand which was almost white. I would not have
been at a loss for things to catalogue.

It suddenly occurred to me that Goon was still alive. It struck me
as obscene that they should put him on trial for his life. He would
be eating, drinking, sleeping, and attending to his wants much as
a house-trained cat might do under the same circumstances. He
would be forced constantly to focus his attention on his bodily
functions. That would cause him to be more aware of himself as a
living thing than he had been before when, in his actions, he would
lose sight of himself. Gradually his mind must have escaped less
and less from the limit of his perceptions. He must have spent hours
and days in measuring distances within his cell.

I remembered one time, after a fight in a bar, I came to consciousness in a hospital. There were screens where the walls should
have been and I smelled iodoform instead of the air that hangs
around a bed where two people have slept. I was living with Cathie
at the time. On returning home things were different. As I wakened
and began to take in my surroundings I realized that the constable
was not there on a chair close by the bed and holding his helmet
by the rim as he had been when suddenly at the hospital, out of
nothing, I came back to my senses, thinking the peak of his helmet

was a star. I remember he was a young man with worried grey eyes and a white, pouchy face. I cannot remember whether he had a black moustache or no moustache at all. I watched him for a time under the rims of my eyelids and then I must have fallen asleep again because when I looked back he was an older man with veined cheeks and with eyebrows as fierce as shrimps and I can remember the buttons on his uniform were very bright, so bright that beyond the pervasive consciousness of my limbs between the clean sheets I counted them, twice at least to be sure I hadn't made a mistake. I forget how many there were.

I was thinking of that, I suppose, because that was my only direct contact with the police when, beyond me, someone said: "Nonsense!" and I was suddenly aware that the trial had begun. There was Goon, a pale-faced man of middle age, in the dock, two policemen behind him, and then the remark – by whom it was spoken I do not know – was followed by silence in the courtroom which gave way gradually to talking in hushed tones, terminated abruptly by the insistent rapping of the judge's hammer. Looking up at him, I had the impression that I was being stared at by a venomous old turtle.

The court became quiet.

A man in a wig was speaking. He seemed pleased with himself. Even in his gown it was obvious that he had an abnormally large bottom. His voice derived something from his adenoids.

The people in court looked more like birds than ever, tilted, an eye glinting, about to peck. I became absorbed in watching them. As the trial proceeded, they were sometimes bored, sometimes tense and feverish, and all the time ridiculous, blobs of expression huddled together, marvelling at the sanctimonious odour of their paid prosecutors.

Throughout the trial, it was quite clear that they were not talking about Goon at all. The victim created in the speeches of

145

the procurator to fit the sea of evidence had nothing to do with any self Goon was conscious of. I was disturbed by the placid way in which they all took it for granted that it was he whom they were talking about. If they condemned *him* they would condemn Goon, and if they hanged him it would be Goon's body they would cut down.

"When you went," they said.

"When you did this or that."

Questions. Off-key. Counterfeit. Loaded.

I had the impression that they wanted things to fit as a man wants to believe in God.

Goon sat looking sullen and afraid. From time to time he was called upon to testify. He did so with a kind of helpless rage, almost tearfully. A woman's voice beside me said that it was easy to cry when you were caught. She was unable to explain what she meant because an usher warned her to be silent.

The courtroom smelled musty, vaguely perfumed, and very little light penetrated from the street through the high-level window. The. lawyers stood up and sat down, sat down and stood up, and a small man in spectacles was explaining that Goon's fingerprints had been on the shoes of the deceased.

"There could be no mistake."

"What?"

"None whatever." From a handkerchief, tilting his little voice out through his pince-nez.

That item of information obsessed me. No doubt the witness went back to his laboratory afterwards. He did not appear again.

Leslie appeared towards the end of the morning. He had recovered the body from the river. "With Joe," he said.

"Joe?"

It is strange to think that I am mentioned in the papers on the proceeding of this trial.

146

"My mate," Leslie said self-consciously, and there was a titter in court. Leslie wore a high white collar above which his sugar-loaf head with its cropped grey hair maintained a startled tilt during his questioning.

He was not asked for his opinion. The Crown ascertained that the woman was dead when she was pulled from the water.

The court was adjourned at the end of the first day. It was quite obvious that the procurator was going to get his conviction. He was a small man, rather self-satisfied, and he seemed to take a personal pleasure in murdering Goon.

I did not feel like returning to the house immediately. Instead, I took a tram to Kelvingrove and walked through the park. I sat on a seat for a long while thinking about nothing in particular. Ella had not been present at the trial. Leslie had come and gone without seeing me. I wondered vaguely whether he had returned to the barge or whether he was a night watchman somewhere or other in the city. I missed Leslie more than I missed Ella. I was glad to be rid of Ella. There were many things I liked about Leslie.

After a while I got up.

I was walking near the tennis courts when two young men and a girl passed me on the footpath. I supposed they were students because they were carrying books under their arms. When they saw me they stopped laughing. It was as though what they were laughing about was too private to be shared with strangers. And then they were past me and laughing again, and the voice of one of the men came back to me, high, artificial, excited, as though he were mimicking someone, and then the girl's laughter again. I turned to watch them.

She was walking between them, swinging a pot-shaped handbag on a long leather strap, in flat shoes and a summer dress, strikingly blonde, her hair rising gracefully from her neck in a ribboned horse-tail. She was slim-hipped and desired obviously by both of them.

They walked out of sight.

I found myself thinking that she could not have been more than twenty-two or so and wondering whether I looked old to her, and then I found myself envying the two young men who escorted her. A feeling almost of despair came over me. I felt a devastating sense of loss for something which I had never had, and it didn't occur to me that that something was a thing which no one ever possesses for the simple reason that it is something which is created in being seen and which exists only for the spectator without whom it could never become an object to tantalize. I was tired and distraught and it did not strike me then that her escorts were even farther than I from the thing for which I felt such an acute sense of loss, infinitely farther from it, because it did not exist for them – their laughter, the swing of her hips, the ribbon, their familiarity, all that. And even if she were the mistress of one of them, I had created the thing for which I felt the sense of loss and it was not anyone else's to be enjoyed. Afterwards I saw that, that it is ludicrous to envy someone a situation which does not exist for him because he is part of it and because it can only be seen, and thus exist, from the outside and then always as a lack.

I did not think that then, but during the night. At that time I was tired and profoundly outraged.

I needed a drink, badly. The social syllogism in which Goon had been unfortunate enough to get himself involved upset me deeply. If any act of mine could have destroyed that syllogism, I should have acted gladly. Go to the police? Confess? In practice I knew it would prove fatal to me. In principle it would have been in an indirect but very fundamental way to affirm the validity of the particular social structure I wished to deny.

A double whisky was more relevant, more fit under the circumstances. I drank two in the nearest bar. As I hadn't eaten since early morning the alcohol had an exaggerated effect upon me. When I left the pub I was feeling slightly tipsy.

I found myself in a large public library with an old number of the *British Medical Journal* open in front of me. I read:

When the first pair were hanged it was my duty to determine the fact of death. As a general rule, on auscultation the heart may be heard beating for about ten minutes after the drop, and on this occasion, when the sounds had ceased, there was nothing to suggest a vital spark. The bodies were cut down after fifteen minutes and placed in an ante-chamber, when I was horrified to hear one of the supposed corpses give a gasp and find him making spasmodic respiratory efforts, evidently a prelude to revival. The two bodies were quickly suspended again for a quarter of an hour longer. The executioner, who was thoroughly experienced, had done his part without a hitch, and the drop given was the regulation one according to individual physique. Dislocation of the neck is the ideal to be aimed at, but, out of all my post-mortem findings, that has proved rather an exception, while in the majority of instances the cause of death was strangulation and asphyxia.

I don't know how long I stared at it before I thrust it away from me across the table. I left it there, not bothering to return it to the desk, and walked blindly out of the library.

When I returned to the flat in Lucien Street, Connie's husband was preparing to go to work. Connie was wrapping his sandwiches in a sheet of newspaper. "Goon Arraigned..." the print said.

"How did it go, Joe?" he said.

"They'll find him guilty," I said.

2

THE FOLLOWING MORNING I woke up late. I hadn't slept much during the night. When I went through to the kitchen Connie was kindling the fire and Bill, the night watchman, was asleep in the cavity bed.

"I didn't wake you," Connie said, as though to explain.

"I'm glad you didn't."

"You not going to the trial today?"

"Yeah, I'll go. In an hour or so." I yawned. "Is there a cup of tea?"

She slapped one in front of me. An eternal teapot on the hob. "What's it like, that trial?"

"It's insane," I said. "It's like a football match. Two teams of lawyers preening themselves like turkey cocks and Goon is the ball."

"It's a bliddy shame," she said. "I'm sorry for him. I was readin' the papers. He says he wasn't even there."

"What the bliddy hell d'ye expect him to say?" Bill's voice came from the bed.

"Shut yer gob and go to sleep!" Connie said.

I shaved carefully, watching the smooth line of my chin appear from under the soap in the mirror. It was after eleven when I left the house.

Once again I found myself in Argyle Street. I almost decided not to go. The verdict was a foregone conclusion. They had created a crime and now they had created a man to fit it. The only disquieting part about the whole freak show was that they would condemn a living creature in deference to the system. There was no doubt about it. The man who was created in the speeches of the procurator was fitted admirably to the crime which the police had invented – a very gratifying thing indeed to see two branches of the public service, the judiciary and the police, work together in such imaginative harmony.

I found myself playing pinball in a dive in Jamaica Street. There were a few people hanging around there at that time in the morning. After lunch I made my way to the courtroom and found the jury had already retired. The newspapermen were there with their cameras. I sat down not far from where I had sat on the previous day and waited for the twelve jurymen (three ladies and nine gentlemen) to return. Their pomposity made them ridiculous. It occurred to me that there might be one amongst them who felt like a murderer. The rest would be protected by their sanctimoniousness.

I can remember no quiet so quiet as that which followed when Mr Justice Parkington had finished saying that never before in his long experience of crime had he felt so justified in awarding the maximum penalty. He said it almost lecherously, and only then was I struck by the fact that the man was quite mad.

Goon was called to attention. Mr Justice Parkington asked him if he had anything to say before sentence was passed on him.

"Just that I am innocent, sir. I swear to God!" he mumbled, without daring to look at the owl who leant forward angrily towards him.

The remark was received in silence. Its meaning appeared to escape everyone. Having said it, Goon seemed to sway from the court's presence. He had to be supported by policemen. I take it that this would have happened even if he had been guilty.

Suddenly a woman's voice cried out: "Now you've done it!" All eyes turned on her, a woman in black, rather stout, weeping into a handkerchief – Mrs Goon. The judge's hammer rapped for

PART THREE · CHAPTER 2

order. People close to her were helping her to her seat, and she was whimpering: "He'd be better dead... he'd be better dead!..."

"Silence in court!"

In the silence which followed, Mr Justice Parkington fitted the black cap neatly to his balding crown and delivered his barbaric sentence in nasal tones. The law, it seemed, required that Goon be hanged by the neck until dead. A day was prescribed. The time, early in the morning. Mr Justice Parkington's denture-shored mouth then uttered the formula that God should have mercy on Goon's soul.

For a moment I wondered whether I was going to stand up and give him the lie. I felt my body tense as a gambler's, a gambler who, just before the last call for bets, is poised in indecision whether or not to throw his whole stake on the red or the black, and who breathes with relief as the *croupier* says: "No more bets." The stake remained in my hand, my life, and I knew that it would never be in the balance again, that Goon had lost and stood now entirely at the mercy of those who had condemned him. My body was in a cold sweat.

The courtroom was silent and grey and heavy with its high ceiling, and the brass lamp brackets on the walls were high up and austere. I tried to hear the noise of the traffic outside on the streets. I wanted badly to hear that, but the walls must have been too thick. And the people were silent except for a slight cough, a rustling of paper, the small scraping of a boot.

I cannot remember how the court broke up. All I know is that suddenly Mr Justice Parkington was gone and the disintegration was already taking place.

ONEWORLD CLASSICS

ONEWORLD CLASSICS aims to publish mainstream and lesser-known European classics in an innovative and striking way, while employing the highest editorial and production standards. By way of a unique approach the range offers much more, both visually and textually, than readers have come to expect from contemporary classics publishing.

CHARLOTTE BRONTË: *Jane Eyre*

EMILY BRONTË: *Wuthering Heights*

ANTON CHEKHOV: *Sakhalin Island*
Translated by Brian Reeve

CHARLES DICKENS: *Great Expectations*

D.H. LAWRENCE: *The First Women in Love*

D.H. LAWRENCE: *The Second Lady Chatterley's Lover*

D.H. LAWRENCE: *Selected Letters*

JAMES HANLEY: *Boy*

JACK KEROUAC: *Beat Generation*

JANE AUSTEN: *Emma*

JANE AUSTEN: *Pride and Prejudice*

JANE AUSTEN: *Sense and Sensibility*

WILKIE COLLINS: *The Moonstone*

GIUSEPPE GIOACCHINO BELLI: *Sonnets*
Translated by Mike Stocks

DANIEL DEFOE: *Robinson Crusoe*

ROBERT LOUIS STEVENSON: *Treasure Island*

GIACOMO LEOPARDI: *Canti*
Translated by J.G. Nichols

OSCAR WILDE: *The Picture of Dorian Gray*

GEOFFREY CHAUCER: *Canterbury Tales*
Adapted into modern English by Chris Lauer

HENRY MILLER: *Quiet Days in Clichy*

NATHANIEL HAWTHORNE: *The Scarlet Letter*

MARY WOLLSTONECRAFT SHELLEY: *Frankenstein*

FRANZ KAFKA: *Letter to My Father*
Translated by Hannah Stokes

BRAM STOKER: *Dracula*

ANN RADCLIFFE: *The Italian*

CALDER PUBLICATIONS

SINCE 1949, JOHN CALDER has published eighteen Nobel Prize winners and around fifteen hundred books. He has put into print many of the major French and European writers, almost single-handedly introducing modern literature into the English language. His commitment to literary excellence has influenced two generations of authors, readers, booksellers and publishers. We are delighted to keep John Calder's legacy alive and hope to honour his achievements by continuing his tradition of excellence into a new century.

ANTONIN ARTAUD: *The Theatre and Its Double*

LOUIS-FERDINAND CÉLINE: *Journey to the End of the Night*

MARGUERITE DURAS: *The Sailor from Gibraltar*

ERICH FRIED: *100 Poems without a Country*

EUGÈNE IONESCO: *Plays*

LUIGI PIRANDELLO: *Collected Plays*

RAYMOND QUENEAU: *Exercises in Style*

ALAIN ROBBE-GRILLET: *In the Labyrinth*

ALEXANDER TROCCHI: *Cain's Book*

To order any of our titles and for up-to-date information about our current and forthcoming publications, please visit our website on:

www.oneworldclassics.com